Unity

Volume 2

A Speculative Anthology

Penned in the City

Also available by Barrio Blues Press

Nation: A Poetry Book by Penned in the City (October 2020)

Unity, Volume 1: A Magical Realism Anthology (December 2020)

Wolf Trek: A Post-Apocalyptic Werewolf Novelette (January 2021)

My Spoken Word Wife: Playing for Keeps (October 2022)

Sojourns (February 2024)

This War (September 2024)

The Teeth of Maggots (March 2025)

Unity

Volume 2

A Speculative Anthology

Edited by
Daniel Brooks
Elaine Marie Carnegie-Padgett
María J. Estrada

BARRIO BLUES PRESS
Chicago 2025

FIRST BARRIO BLUES PRESS EDITION, MARCH 2025
Unity, Volume 2: A Speculative Anthology
Copyright © 2025 by María J. Estrada
Book design by María J. Estrada
Cover design © Andjela Vujic
Cover art © Norbert Somosi
Internal art © pngtree.com

Published by Barrio Blues Press
Chicago, IL 60609
Barriobluespress.com
(312) 685-1602
Barrio Blues Press Trade Paperback:
ISBN: 978-1-954444-05-8

"The Exchange Student" © 2001 Kurt Newton. First published in *Earwig Flesh Factory*. Reprinted by permission of the author.

"Communion" © 2002 Vonnie Winslow Crist. First published in *Rivers of Stars*. Reprinted by permission of the author.

"Box 27" © 2016 Kevin Lauderdale. First published in *Nature*. Reprinted by permission of the author.

"Encuentros con la Llorona" © 2022 Carmen Baca. First published in *Bella Collector of Cuentos*. Reprinted by permission of the author.

Printed in the United States of America.

iv

For the people of Palestine and all those in
war-torn countries.

Contents

Introduction

by María J. Estrada

When the first volume of *Unity* was produced in 2020, we were a divided country. Now, as we launch *Unity, Volume 2: a Speculative Anthology*, we are even more divided with demonstrations in almost every state, with participants angry at the cost of living rising and the current president signing executive orders that are destroying our democracy and racial unity. However, there is hope in the unity of these demonstrators and common people joining to oppose attacks on our democracy.

Although this volume is not a political one, the concepts of unity or dis-unity have the reader reflect on their humanity and what it means to come together as part of the human race. The anthology begins with "To the Moon and Back" by Beth Patterson where an imprisoned magical creature struggles to be set free and how the kindness of strangers can make a difference in a struggle. "We Aren't Salem Here," by Isabelle Palerma narrates the tragic story of two sisters being accused of witchcraft, demonstrating how unity can be used to harm others. Each story offers a unique interpretation of the anthology's theme that will keep the reader wondering what comes next.

Similarly, the poetry offers both hope and a lack of as in the poem "The End of the World" by Michelle Chermaine Ramos where she writes:

The stars began to die.

The sun came out from the west.
The cat played the fiddle.
Tadpoles sprang from a cuckoo's nest.
Hot dogs started barking.
The sea washed itself away.

"Brain-Machine Interface" by S Jade Path has the reader consider the possibility of unity:

There is a space between moments
Between yes, no, and maybe
Where breath waits, and time stops
It's in this moment that we connect
Where our collective being exists
Before the world intervenes
Before conditioning before fear
Before hate before discord
These moments exist
Without division

That moment "Where our collective being exists" is crucial to the concept of Unity. Many of the poems embody this spirit.

The artwork is gorgeous, offering the same contrast of what happens if we come together or fail to do so. "Root 66" by Belinda Subraman shows a mass of people intertwined with each other, their haunting, happy faces challenging us to wonder whether they are happy or distressed. "We are the Landfill" by Jai Caldwell offers a compelling graphic of bodies intertwined with each other in harmony around the earth or a planet of unknown origin. The artwork is beautifully inspired by the theme of Unity.

The editorial board and I are grateful to the members of *Penned in the City: A Creative Writing Group for All* for their amazing work. We owe a special debt to Andjela Vujic and Norbert Somosi for uplifting this anthology through their graphic designs, which are just as wonderful as the works found here. All of the writers and artists and people who made this anthology a reality *are* making a better world possible as the proceeds for this book are going to *Doctors Without Borders*.

FICTION

To the Moon and Back

by Beth Patterson

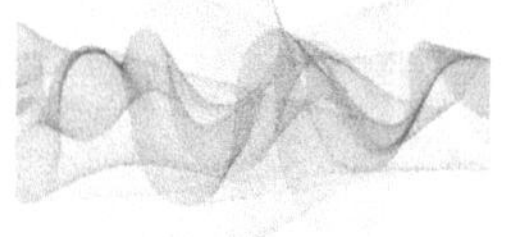

She was self-conscious about the sound of her plodding, ungainly footsteps. Even though she'd managed to shed the bell strapped around her neck, she still felt inelegant. Yet Clara refused to stop. Her body was weary, but she had much to ruminate on. She was almost always ruminating, for she was, after all, a cow.

Her passenger shifted positions, wrapping her long wings more tightly around Clara's neck. The poor goose was half dead, but her wounds were bound tightly enough for Clara to cling to hope. The bird's owner had thought that if he sliced his goose open, he'd be able to retrieve enough gold to satisfy the immediate fix he had come to crave. Only for Clara's sharp ears and impulsive strafing would he be none the wiser.

They were quite the pair: the goose who once laid golden eggs riding on the cash cow, and their survival would be defiance of human greed. Clara didn't know where to go, for most of her travels had been on a wagon. All she knew was that she had to keep on trudging.

As the familiar turf faded into unknown territory, the landmarks morphed into a comforting darkness. No shadows to play tricks on Clara's mind, this non-place had the peaceful ambiance of a starlit sky. The road they took became a wide ribbon of time and space, a weft and warp of choice and chance woven tightly enough to support the cow's weight. It wound its way through the void, sparkling nebulas flashing in all directions. *This is where dreams go to die and become reborn,* Clara mused. She did not question how she knew this. Beasts were better than humans when it came to instinctive assessments of the mystical.

The ribbon morphed into a dirt road, and fertile land materialized from the coruscating space before them. A signpost that read UNSTABLE FABLES marked this new terrain. It didn't seem like much of a promised land, but Clara figured that it was better than their previous dwelling. The thud of her footsteps fell into a cadence as a barely audible chant fell upon her ears:

> *With a thunkety-thud*
> *And stained with blood,*
> *She takes the dark dirt road*
> *With caution and care*
> *Is this a snare,*

Or asylum for her load?

The citizens seemed to be comprised of more animals than people, which was a good sign. But many of them were frustrated. Off to the side of the road, Clara saw a fox leaping at some hanging grape vines just out of his reach and then declaring them sour. Down the path was a barn with a manger that would have been a good source of hay, but a snarling dog atop the food kept the cow at bay. A young boy dashed across the path, hollering that a wolf had attacked his flock of sheep, but he was chortling to himself, as if this were all a great joke.

This was no place for them, where they might suffer in order to teach lessons of morality. Clara kept on trudging.

The village ahead dissolved into the void once more, and the dancing lights of entropy against darkness were soothing. The path resumed its space-time ribbon form. It didn't matter to Clara if little made sense here. She just had to keep up the steady pace, which gave her more time to reflect on her decision to flee her former life.

Her handler had never let her eat enough for her to be productive, but was constantly berating her that she would never be as successful as her red-spotted rival, Ermintrude. His hints at her impending death grew more frequent each day, and Clara had secretly decided to break out as soon as the timing was right. But when she heard shrieks and honks as the farmer next door attempted to disembowel his goose, she knew that it was now or never. She'd kicked down the fencepost, escaped her prison, and charged the murderous man and his wife. It was a stroke of luck that Clara hadn't gored anyone. Equally fortuitous was how the farmwife's apron had caught on one of her horns, serving as a makeshift bandage for the wounded bird once they'd put some distance between themselves and the farms. Lacking opposable thumbs, the cow had still been handy with her teeth and lips for emergency first aid.

The ribbon beneath her feet changed from soft earth to cobblestones, snapping the cow out of her reverie. She looked to the horizon to see signs of civilization. The next signpost read GRIM FATES. That didn't sound inviting either, although the scenery was more striking. Her hooves clopped on the road in a pattern, and once again, she thought she imagined a rhyme:

> *With a clippety-clop*
> *She makes a stop,*
> *Her senses more discerning*
> *Will they let her in*
> *As an equal and friend,*

Or a tool for human learning?

Off in the distance rose a castle with an ivory tower. They didn't seem like they'd be able to help the long-haired woman trapped in its high loft. The gingerbread house looked too good to be true. Oddest of all was the vegetation, namely a beanstalk that grew so high, it disappeared into the clouds. Clara wondered how high a living creature might be able to go.

This was no place for them, where they might suffer in order to teach lessons of courage. Clara kept on trudging.

The darkness enveloped the two beasts once more. The cow wondered if there was a place for them in the constellations. After all, in her world there was already a bull and a swan lighting up the patterns of the night sky, so why now a cow and a goose? As if to answer her unspoken question, the twinkling lights in the void shifted and repositioned themselves.

Darkness gave way to warm sunshine, and the ribbon became a solid meadow. No hard ground met her hooves, just a lovely field of grass that swished up to her knees and hocks. As much as she dearly wanted to stop and graze, the goose's critical condition urged her on. Her rhythm sped up, and with it the voices:

With a swishety-swish
She makes a wish,
Soft grass beneath her feet
Is there hope and a chance
In these verdant plants,
Fit for a cow to eat?

The next sign was almost worn away, but she could see traces of something like MADAM HEART MOTHER. It was not really a village as much as a clearing that revealed a ramshackle cottage, a large pumpkin shell, and a giant shoe. The metal chimney pipe at the highest eyelet puffed the cheerful, pungent smoke of a turf fire. A door set in the toe swung open to reveal a spry old woman.

The lively crone was dressed in rags of every color of reborn dreams. The bun of her hair was silver and purple, swirled like a peppermint. She picked up her skirts as she hurried toward the newcomers, revealing striped socks and short leather boots with brass buckles. This was clearly someone more concerned with figments than fineries.

She took one look at the wary cow and the wounded bird and tisk-tisked to herself. "Oh, you poor darlings. What have we here?" Her voice was the creak of a leather-bound book with the singsong cadence of a rocking horse.

"Can you help Goosie?" asked Clara. "We need a place to settle down, and I'm trying to escape butchery, but first I need to try to save my friend." She wasn't sure that she could trust humans, but this was the first one who had ever spoken kindly to her.

The old woman gathered the bird in her arms and said, "Let's go inside. I'll get you some food, we'll tend to your friend, and you can tell me all about it."

"Are you a witch?"

"Not exactly. I am a keeper of rhymes, some of which might contain a whiff of magic. They call me by many names, including Madam Heart Mother, Susie Shoesquatter, and Mère L'Oie."

Some other animals had already made themselves at home in the shoe. There was a black hen, a couple of dogs, and a cat that was trying to open a violin case. Through the window, Clara could even see a mouse that had busied itself with nesting in a tall grandfather clock.

The old woman scuttled down the hall into a bedroom. She tenderly laid the goose on her bed, heedless of the drying blood smearing her quilted bedspread. She unbound the dressing and uttered a chant:

"Goosie-goosie-gander
No longer wander

Safe from the farmer

And all further slander."

The bird gave a sigh and managed to tuck itself into a nesting position, head under her wing.

"When she wakes, I'll give her some warm mash to give her back her strength," said the old woman, pulling a stool into a corner and making room for her bovine visitor to kneel and rest. She disappeared down the hallway for a moment.

She said that she's sometimes known as 'Mère L'Oie,' thought the cow. *Could this be the same woman that some call 'Mother Goose'?*

The crone returned with a trough of oats for Clara as if she expected bovine visitors on a daily basis. "Now tell me, dear," said Madam Heart Mother, settling down on the stool. "Why would anyone want to slaughter such a beautiful cow?"

"I stopped being productive."

"You could no longer give milk?"

Clara shook her large head. "No, I never chose to have any offspring. I was a classically trained singer, but once I reached a certain age, my owner—also my manager—said that people would be more in the market for a young heifer. I was no longer attractive, so he signed a contract that would permit him to turn me into steaks and burgers. My legacy would have been more valuable once I was dead."

"I know this village you speak of, and I've heard your name," said Madam Heart Mother as the ravenous cow munched her oats. "You traveled a long way to get here, Clara, which takes stamina. You're quite the athlete."

"Athlete?" This was a new one for the tired animal. She'd seen oxen laboring in the fields, but that was a job, not a sport.

"Listen, my child. It takes maintaining physical skills to hold a music career. If you play an instrument, you are an athlete. If you are a singer, you are an athlete. Why, I'll bet you could make it over the moon in a single leap."

Mildly irritable from fatigue and confusion, Clara opened her mouth to dismiss the woman. But the human lady seemed so genuine, that the cow decided to humor her instead. After all, this was her best chance of finding asylum. "All right, since you insist . . ." Clara backed out of the bedroom, clopped down the hall, and out of the giant shoe.

Back outside, the passage of time had turned the sky into a twilight tapestry. The sun had already set, and constellations she recognized were beginning to appear. The waxing crescent moon crooked like a beckoning finger, and Clara fixed her gaze upon it. With a snort, she willed her aching body into a gallop. Gaining momentum, she gathered herself for a spring and pushed upward with all her might.

As all four hooves left the ground, the most peculiar thing happened. She rose in the air and kept rising in her own powerful trajectory. The cow tucked her forelegs to her chest and pointed her nose at the heavens like a streamlined missile.

The earth got smaller and smaller behind her, and before she knew it, Clara had broken through the atmosphere. She felt bracingly cold, but she did not freeze or suffer from a lack of oxygen. The moon loomed ahead as big as a pie plate, then a bass drumhead, and finally taking up her entire field of vision. She was transfixed by its forgotten seas, its craters an ancient code in the diary of a long-forgotten big bang. There were even signs of human trespassing, such as flags and footprints. *But no one will intrude in this place I'll be landing . . . if I make it back to the realm of Madam Heart Mother,* she thought.

Instead of making a lunar landing, Clara floated effortlessly over the pale, craggy sphere. Her orbit took her past the dark side of the moon, and she gazed out into infinite space.

For a moment, the stars, rumored to be long dead, flared in tribute. She soaked up a wash of light, and for a brief ecstatic moment, she was one of them. What part of some celestial grand design was she a part of? Taurus? Or was she part of some alien constellation in cosmic layout from an entirely different perspective? She drifted downward, leaving the moon behind, and then the memory of the kind old woman kicked the gravitational pull into effect.

As she commenced her return to the earth, blue and dappled with clouds, she saw her own world from a new viewpoint. She took in the sight of entire continents and seas. Sinking faster, she caught the crinkled and twisted splendor of mountains and rivers from a vantage point never before seen through bovine eyes. Finally, her descent slowed, and she could make out villages and the little clearing where the old woman and her friends dwelled. The shoe stood out like a landmark on a game board.

Clara landed as lightly as a feather. Cheering erupted all around her as the residents of the giant shoe gathered to marvel at her. The cat managed to open the violin case and played some impressive licks—*Tchaikovsky Four, fourth movement, not bad,* she marveled. One of the dogs cackled with delight, and no one even cared that some of the cutlery and plates had escaped together.

And Goosie, her beloved companion, waddled out of the doorway, still weak but very much alive. The bird scuttled over to Clara who knelt in the grass. The goose stretched her wings across the cow's neck in a universally understood embrace.

Madam Heart Mother danced toward them in a swish of skirts. "You are now Clara de la Lune. This is where you belong," said the old woman, beaming. "And as for your goose friend, she will also spend the rest of her days here, for I am mother to her kind."

"Here we can thrive, where our existence will protect the hearts of the innocent," said an oddly familiar voice. Clara looked down and saw that it was Goosie who had spoken. It was then Clara realized that the voice she'd heard on their journey had belonged to the bird. "Geese are sacred guardians of children's rhymes," continued her healing companion. "You and I are living verses now, and for your heroism, I love you to the moon and back."

With a clarion honk strong enough to be heard by all, Goosie chanted:

With a lunge and a leap
And the world asleep,
The cow jumped over the moon
She shone like a blaze,
Every star was amazed
And her deeds are forever a boon

Echoes

by Paula Shablo

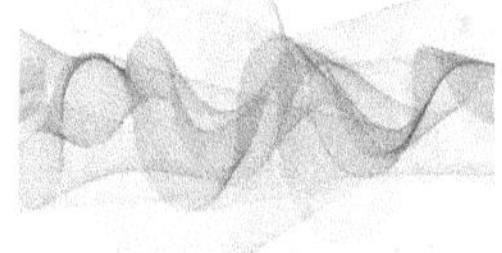

Billy stood with his mother near the edge of the precipice, looking down into the valley below. Pinion pines, fir trees, and aspens, some tall enough to reach out and touch—if he didn't mind a great fall, that is—marched their way down to the edge of the river; and far, far across from them, he could see the rocky side of a mountain.

He cupped his hands around his mouth. "Hello!" he called. "I am Billy!" He waited for his echo to come bouncing back to him across the valley.

Nothing.

Perplexed, he looked up at his mother. "What's wrong with my echo?" he asked.

Helena smiled and put an arm around his shoulder, patting him reassuringly. "Oh," she said, "Snow probably muffles the sound."

"Snow? What sn—?" Billy turned, gesturing at the valley below. He stopped talking abruptly and stared, jaw agape. Snow covered every surface. In the bright sunlight, it sparkled extravagantly from treetops and mountainside. The river below was frozen. A gust of wind blew sheets of it from the pines, casting iridescent flashes across the valley below. The colors were blindingly brilliant, and Billy gasped in delight.

How had he missed the snow a moment before? He would have sworn—

"The world is full of beauty," Helena sighed extravagantly. "I forgot about that."

"What?"

Helena smiled distractedly and pulled Billy into her arms for a long hug. Billy hugged back. It was nice to get a hug from his mother. She usually wasn't still long enough for an enduring hug like this one.

"Why don't echoes work in the snow?"

"I don't know, baby. Maybe they do. Maybe I'm wrong."

Billy cupped one hand around his mouth, still hugging his mother with the other arm. "Hello?" he called.

There was still no answering echo.

He didn't like that. His brow creased, a deep frown of consternation darkening his features. "Where are we?" he asked.

"Here."

"Yeah, but—" He craned his neck, staring up at his mother, suddenly suspicious. "Where is here?"

"Isn't it lovely?"

It was. The snow glittered and flashed, the treetops swayed, colors splashed across the ice on the river below, and everything was gorgeous.

They stood looking, watching the snow blow in whirling dervishes as the wind changed directions. Billy frowned again and looked up at his mother. Her chestnut hair hung to her waist, unmoving. His own hair was still.

It was so very odd. Their hair should be thrashing around their heads. Not only that, but he realized he didn't feel cold.

He was trying not to be scared. "Mom?" he asked. "Are we going soon?"

"I think so."

Billy looked around. There was no road that he could see, and no footpath, either. "Where's the car?"

"Oh," Helena remarked, "It's around here somewhere, I guess."

"I don't remember . . ." Billy's voice trailed off. He felt more than uneasy. Nothing was right. "How did we get up here? Did we walk?"

He was wearing an old Alice Cooper t-shirt that had belonged to his father. It was his favorite and was nearly transparent with age. He had on cargo shorts and ratty old huaraches. He should have been freezing.

"Mom?" He had so many questions! But before he could ask—

"Billy?"

Billy turned to see who had called his name. His great-grandparents stood a few feet away. "Gigi Ma! Grampy!" He pulled out of his mother's embrace and ran to them.

Helena gave a low moan of despair and lowered her empty arms to her sides.

Gigi hugged Billy tightly. Grampy feigned offering a handshake—very manly—and then pulled him in for a fierce hug, too. "Where have you been?" Billy demanded. "I missed you so much!"

Gigi looked over at her granddaughter who hadn't moved. "Helena," she said, nodding slightly.

"Hello, Grandma." She looked at Grampy. "Hello, Grandpa. You look well."

"We are," Grampy replied.

"Oh, Helena," Gigi sighed.

Billy watched this exchange with some alarm.

"I wondered who would come," Helena said and smiled. "I'm glad it's you."

"Mom?" Billy pulled away from Grampy and started running back to his mother. No matter how fast he ran, she never got any closer. "Mom, what's happening?" He raised his arms, reaching for her.

"No going backward," Grampy said. Billy stopped running and turned toward his great-grandfather, and he was *right there*. Billy hadn't moved an inch! "We can only go forward from here."

"We?" Billy looked back at his mother. "Mom?"

"I love you, Billy." Still, she didn't move. She stood at the very edge, hands at her sides, and she smiled at him. "Remember that. Go with Gigi and Grampy, now."

"Go? Go where?" Billy could feel tears prickling the backs of his eyes, as he swallowed hard. Wasn't she coming, too?

Helena looked at her grandmother. "Take him quickly," she said quietly. "I don't want him to . . . to see what's next."

She turned to her grandfather. "I never did know anything," she said. "I never could answer his questions. Tell him about echoes."

Her eyes were filled with tears. She blinked, and they spilled down her cheeks. She smiled brilliantly at them. "I love you," she said. "I—" She turned away then and stared out across the valley. "I love you all forever."

Billy's hands were clasped by his great-grandparents, and suddenly they were rising. Up, up; further and further away; his mother seemed to be shrinking below him. "Mom? Mooooooooommmmm!"

"It's fine, son."

Billy stared up into Grampy's face. "No, it's not! It's not fine! Why can't she come, too?"

"*She* knows why," Gigi said quietly.

Billy stared down, no longer able to make out more than an anonymous figure below. "Is she waving?"

"Of course."

"I can't see her!"

"No more looking back," Gigi said. "Look ahead, Billy. See?"

The snow was gone.

Green grass and trees filled the landscape. Flowers were in bloom. The air was fragrant with their tantalizing scents.

A chunky corgi was waddling toward them and started running when she saw Billy's face. "Bunny!" Billy cried. "Oh, Bunny!" He knelt on the grass, and the dog leapt into his arms and licked his face. "Hello, girl! I missed you!"

After a happy reunion, the boy and dog raced ahead of the old couple. Grampy looked back, in spite of his own advice to Billy.

"Is she gone?" Gigi asked.

Grampy sighed. "Not yet."

"Oh, Helena!" Gigi's voice was filled with dismay. Grampy took her hand, squeezing gently. They followed Billy, shaking their heads. There was nothing more to be done, now that they had retrieved the boy.

No more looking back.

Far below, Helena stood at the edge of the precipice.

Should she jump?

Wouldn't that be redundant?

She wondered who would be coming for her. She cupped her hands around her mouth and called "Hello!"

Warbling voices echoed back at her: "Helena! Helena!"

She shuddered. Dear God, what had she done?

The Guy with a Life Mission

by Christopher T. Dabrowski

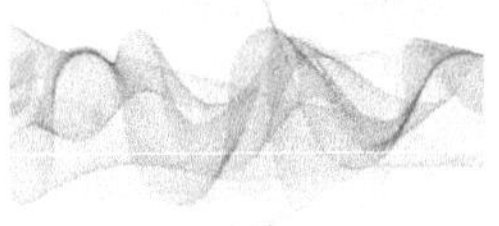

He loved to fight for the rights of the oppressed. He thought that his life mission was to be good.

He saved animals, helped the poor, and chained himself to the trees. He was protecting, saving, and helping.

People admired him. Everyone wanted to be his friend. Women dreamt about him. Then everything changed. The world became good.

But instead of being happy, he felt sad. No one got hurt, there was no one to save.

He felt unnecessary, even though people admired and loved him.

He decided that he would change too: From now on, he would be bad!

The Friends

by Christopher T. Dabrowski

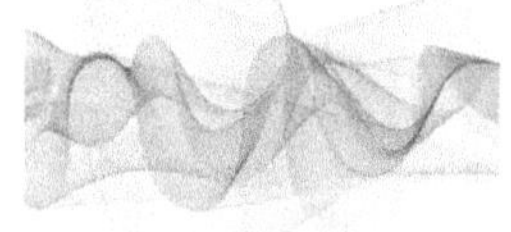

I have visited a friend today. Just like that, to chat, because in my life a lot has changed lately.

"I asked her to marry me," I confessed to Jozef.

"And what?" he asked.

"She refused."

"You must be devastated."

"Come on, I took that hand myself."

I pulled out a limb from behind my coat.

"Oh shit, you've got balls, man!" he praised me. "What about the rest?"

"In the fridge. That's enough . . . for a honeymoon.

We drank vodka and gave him a hand as a gift.

The Cosmic Dilemmas

by Christopher T. Dabrowski

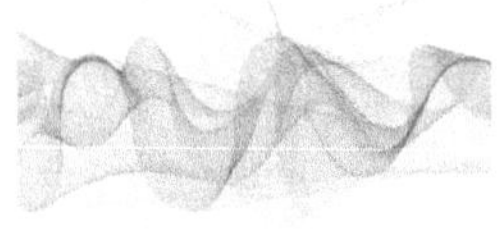

Two Xerrans on intergalactic spacecraft XC705:

"Shall we tell them?" asked Ghu.

"What for?" Ghi said.

"Well, they should know."

"That they don't exist? Why would they know that?"

"Wouldn't you want to know?"

"No, I wouldn't."

"By the way, it's funny that five years have passed since 2012 and none of them have suspected anything."

"It's good that we uploaded the minds of all the humans into the system before the end of the planet."

"How splendid that we have done the simulation of Earth."

Two Meenaans on the inter-dimensional ship Naamaaste:

"Are we gonna tell Xerrans they're gone?"

The Meeting

by Christopher T. Dabrowski

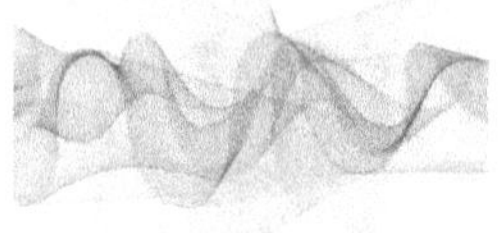

Somebody was at the door. I didn't expect anyone, but I opened it.

The old man invited himself in.

The doorbell rang.

It was some blond beauty.

Then an Asian man marched in.

Jesus . . . I thought.

Jesus appeared at the door. Then a clown and some old lady. Eventually, my psychiatrist came.

"It was difficult to gather you together, but it finally happened," he said. "You must know that you all live in the same body."

I felt weak.

"We are going to vote now to choose which personality will stay here. I will ask the rest to leave this man's head."

Remote Control

by Dawn DeBraal

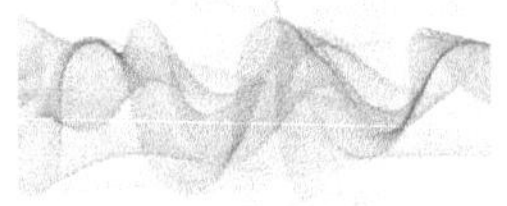

Billy Rayburn skated along the sidewalk past the signs that showed a picture of a skateboard with a large red circle and a line going through it. He was that kid who ignored the rules; instead, he loved bending them to the point of breaking. He was going along at a good clip when he hit a huge glob of gum on the sidewalk. It caught in the wheels of his Santa Cruz skateboard, stopping it instantly and throwing him forward. He windmilled his arms, shouting to the man in front of him, "Watch out," and then found himself riding the man's legs down to the sidewalk.

The man in the trench coat turned and scowled at him, running off. Billy tried to shake off the hard fall when he saw something on the ground. It resembled a remote control.

"Hey! Mister, you dropped something," Billy called out as he picked it up. The remote was nearly weightless. The small metallic body curved in his hand. There was only one button from what he could tell. Billy wondered what the remote did.

He searched the crowd around him. The guy was long gone. Oh well. He'd take it home and find out on the internet what it was. Maybe he could sell it. Make enough money for a better skateboard.

He picked up the Santa Cruz, turning it over. To his disgust, gum had intricately woven itself into the front wheel. How could anyone have had that amount of gum in their mouth at once? It grossed him out, but he picked at it until his front wheel was free. The old man came out of the shop where he had fallen.

"Are you okay, Billy?"

"Yeah, only my pride is hurt," he responded.

"Shouldn't be on the sidewalk." Mr. Antonio the shopkeeper, said sullenly. Billy didn't wait for any more of his sass and knew the guy would probably call his dad. He started to drive the board forward while the man called for him to get off the sidewalk. Billy laughed as he rounded the corner.

When he came to the skateboard park, Billy sat down to look again at the object he'd found on the sidewalk.

"Hey! Creep." Larry was supposed to be a friend, but he was more of an acquaintance. They only hung out together when they got to the skate park. Larry knew some pretty great tricks and showed Billy how to do them. Billy knew that part of Larry got off being an instructor to his friend.

But there was only one way to learn tricks, and that was from someone else. You couldn't watch YouTube and do the trick at the park.

"Hey, Larry." Billy tried to get the object back into his pocket.

"Whatcha got there?" Larry questioned, grabbing the remote out of his hand.

"I don't know. I slammed into a guy, and he dropped it and ran off." Larry hefted it in his hand.

"It's got to be fake or empty. It doesn't weigh anything. What does it do?"

"I was trying to figure that out when you grabbed it from me." Larry pushed the button and disappeared. The remote clattered to the ground.

Billy jumped up, looking around. Where had he gone? He eyeballed the remote. Stooping to pick it up, he was surprised by the heat that came from the small instrument. Billy dropped it quickly in his pocket, then skated out of the park as fast as he could for home. He needed to find out what happened to his friend. It was like he was vaporized or something. He would research what this thing was on the internet.

After searching for an hour, Billy's knowledge of what he had found was still a mystery. Billy knew he didn't want to push the button; otherwise, what had happened to Larry most likely would happen to him. He tossed the object in his dresser drawer and went down for dinner when his dad called him.

"Billy, I got a call from Mr. Antonio. Were you skateboarding on the sidewalk again?"

"Oh, Dad, he's such a fuddy-duddy. I went just a little way down the sidewalk."

"I don't want to have to pay for a ticket. You stay off the sidewalk, or I won't let you go to the park on your own anymore." He knew his dad was lying because there was one thing his dad hated more than going to Billy's school, and that was sitting there watching his son try and break his neck on the halfpipe.

"Okay, Dad," was all Billy said and dug into his macaroni and cheese. After proving he did his homework, Billy removed the wheels from his skateboard and pulled out the bearings. He cleaned each wheel thoroughly, making sure the gum was gone. With a couple of drops of bearing oil, he expertly put the board back together. Billy would try the park again tomorrow. He heard the phone ring, and his dad called up the steps, "Did you see Larry today?"

"Yeah, I didn't talk to him, but I thought I saw him. I turned around, and he was gone." Billy called back down. He could hear his dad on the phone, no doubt with Larry's parents. It still bothered him what happened to his friend, but how could he explain what it was he saw? It defied explanation.

Larry's face was plastered on posters all over town. Billy was freaking out. It was only a matter of time before the cops questioned him. Why did he say he'd seen Larry the day he went missing? It had been three days now.

Looking out the window of his bedroom, Billy saw him, the cop. He was coming to question him. He knew it. Billy panicked. He hadn't done anything but find something that Larry pushed the button on and disappeared right in front of him. Once again, Billy felt he was in trouble and panicked. He rummaged around in his drawer and found the remote.

As the doorbell rang, he pushed the button on the remote control. Only the small metal instrument lay on the floor in Billy's room.

When his dad came into his room with the police, he was shouting.

"Billy!" there was nothing but dirty clothes on his floor. His father scratched his head.

"He was here. I don't know where he went." The officer picked up the remote.

"What is this?"

"I don't know. I never saw it before." The officer pushed the button to see if the remote ran a sound system in Billy's room and vaporized. The remote fell to the floor.

"What the hell?" Mr. Rayburn shouted as he grabbed the remote. It was hot to the touch.

Billy plunged down a dark hole, landing on a hard surface in a dark room with an awesome swirling vortex at the end. Standing in front of the tunnel was his friend.

"Larry!" he shouted. Larry stood mesmerized by the swirling mass in front of them.

"It's a wormhole. We can time travel," Larry called back to him.

"How do you know that?"

"I've read just about everything ever written about them. I know this is what this is. That remote takes you here, but how you navigate it, I can't say for sure."

Both boys turned around from the grunt behind them, seeing the police officer getting up from the ground. The cop drew his gun.

"It's just us, Larry and Billy," Billy shouted back. The officer reholstered his weapon as he walked up to the boys.

"It's a wormhole!" he said, surprised.

"Am I the only one who doesn't know about these things?" Billy asked in exasperation.

"That's what I think," Larry responded.

"This thing can take us through time, but how do we control it? Where did you get that remote control?"

Billy spoke up, "I accidentally ran into a guy on the sidewalk the other day. He ran off but dropped it. Larry pushed the button and disappeared. When I saw you at my door, I knew I was in trouble, so I pushed the button and ended up here."

The officer already had his flashlight out, checking the area.

"It appears to be a waiting room. We are on a platform within the wormhole. I wonder if it's something like a train station?"

"I've been here only a short time, but nothing has stopped," Larry offered.

"Larry, you've been gone for three days," Billy responded.

"Three days? Time stands still here. It feels as if I have only been here a few minutes."

"So, you are saying back home, time keeps moving, but here we are in limbo?" Billy asked.

The officer nodded his head, "I wonder how old this is. I read that it is impossible to return to a time before the wormhole was formed. If we were to enter into it, would we go back to our time... or who knows?"

The officer came closer to the swirling vortex. Billy called for the cop to stop, but he didn't listen. The officer reached his hand out at the end of the platform as far as he could stretch.

Then he shouted as the vortex took him in. He was gone in a flash. Both boys screamed.

"What happened? Where is he?" Billy shouted.

"I don't know. He could be back home, or he could be lost in time. Everything I've ever read has been a theory. No one has ever seen an actual wormhole, at least none has ever been documented as being real."

Billy had a new-found respect for Larry. He wasn't as stupid as Billy thought originally. At least the guy read a book now and then. "So, what do we do now?" Billy asked.

Larry was on his hands and knees searching the floor and the walls. "Try and find some answers." Billy got down on all fours. He felt like a mime as he put one hand in front of the other going around the room when he heard a sucking sound, and an invisible door slid open. There was a remote control.

"I think I've found it!" Billy cried in excitement. Larry came over, looking at what he had in his hand.

"So, do we try?" Billy's hands were shaking. Would this bring them back to their world, and if not, where would they end up?

"You know when we vaporize, we lose the control. How about you hang onto me, and I put this thing in my pocket so it can't get lost? I mean, it would come with us, right?"

"I don't know," Larry said shakily. "Someone had to put that control in the wall. Are there other portals we will be sent to? And how do we know when we get back to the Bakersville portal?" It was a good question. It was not like there was a sign. How did they know if they weren't already at the Bakersville portal? Maybe if they hit the remote, they would find themselves back in the town, or perhaps they would find themselves further away. The two just sat there, unable to come to a decision. Either way, there were risks and possible death.

"Well, we know when we use the remote, it safely transports us somewhere," Larry said quietly. Billy was thinking along those lines, himself. But what happened to the cop? Did he survive jumping into the fray?

"What do you think we should do?" Billy asked without conviction. They were up against a wall.

"What if we jump into the hole and push the remote?" Larry suggested. "Maybe that's what it's for."

"Why would we do that?"

"I don't know. But we could stand here forever, or make a decision, even if it's a bad one."

Billy's finger hovered over the button. Larry wrapped his arms around Billy's waist.

"Let's do both, jump and hit the remote at the same time. On a count of three." Larry started the countdown. "One, two, and he pushed Billy and him into the wormhole before he got to three. Billy slammed the remote in his pocket.

"You jerk!" He was so pissed at his friend. They felt like they were falling, and suddenly a ship with an open top slammed down around them. They were dragged through the wormhole to the unknown. Would they find the cop? Would they end up in Bakersville, or would they crash somewhere and never be found? Brilliant colors circled around the ship. Billy felt sick, just like he did on the tilt-a-whirl. The visual was like that of a 3D Virtual Reality. He only played it once and was ill for the rest of the day. He closed his eyes and told Larry to let go of him, which Larry did.

"Man, this is so awesome." Larry was a freak of nature. He wasn't afraid of anything.

The smell. Ammonia! The ship was on fire!

"We need to get out of here!" Billy screamed, trying to find a lever or a button to get the top off the ship.

"No, it will kill us. Don't you smell it? Ammonia. The ship is the only thing that is keeping us from suffocating. Larry grabbed his friend around the arms and held Billy down.

"Get off of me, you freak!" Billy said, panicking.

"He's coming to!" The EMT worker said, waving the smelling salts under Billy's nose. Mr. Antonio said he called Billy's dad, who was on the way.

"That was quite a spill that boy took. Hit his head on the sidewalk." The officer standing behind the medic said. Billy coughed and jerked. Larry was there, too.

"Where am I?"

"When you didn't come to the park, I came to find you," Larry answered. Billy was confused. "I found you passed out on the sidewalk. Mr. Antonio called an ambulance. It looks like you got a bunch of gum stuck in the front wheel and went off the front of the board."

Billy sat up, overwhelmed with the head rush. He watched his dad pull up to the curb.

"Are you alright?"

Billy nodded, yes.

The EMT explained Billy hit his head and should go to the hospital, but that his dad could transport him now that he was alert and awake. Mr. Rayburn agreed he would take Billy to the emergency room. Larry grabbed the skateboard.

"I'll clean it up for you and drop it off at your house. Take it easy, Billy." Larry skated off.

Billy stood up, walked wobbly to the car, and climbed into the back seat. His dad kept asking if he was okay.

"Yeah, I'm fine, just a headache, and my face hurts." His dad threw a handkerchief in the back seat.

"Wipe off the blood on your neck." Billy rubbed his neck and came away with blood. He went to hand it back to his dad.

"Keep it," his dad said

"Can you open the window?" Billy asked. His dad pushed the lock, and the window rolled down. Billy felt the fresh breeze on his face. It made him feel a little better. He went to put the handkerchief in his pocket, and then he felt it. He pulled out the remote control. They were crossing over the river. Billy flung the remote control as far as he could out the window.

"Did you just throw something out?" his dad asked crossly.

"No, a big dragonfly came through the window. I slapped him back outside." His dad rolled up the window as they neared the end of the bridge. Billy's mouth dropped open when he saw a poster with "Missing Teen" in large letters. Underneath the announcement, Billy watched incredulously as Larry's face faded off the poster on the pole.

Chili and Cacao

by Pani Loh

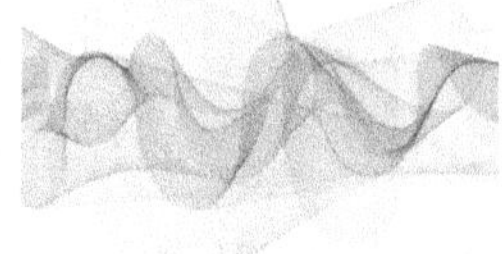

The soup simmered and the aroma of garlic and chili filled the kitchen. I chopped the coriander with firm sharp movements; my brown, red-stained hands were now speckled with green. There was shouting outside and the sound of electric saws cutting the trees rattled the windows.

The key to our ancestral house fell off my belt.

"Alma, it's nearly 1 o'clock!" shouted Jorge.

"Yes! I'll be ready," I said, turning from the stove to pick up the key.

Why did he always have to speak with such urgency? He knew I was never late. Making a meal for twenty wasn't a problem for me. Wasn't that why they were coming here for lunch? That—and my reputation for making tasty, *picante* meals.

It was my pleasure. I knew that the village saw Jorge as the long-suffering husband of the sharp-tongued food magician, who insisted on wearing clothes from an old time. They didn't know that each night after Jorge unplaited my hair, I pulled off his boots and bathed his aching feet in hot water, infused with garden flowers and herbs.

Jorge loved this, especially when followed by a foot massage. He worked hard each day growing the chilies and unloading the cocoa bean deliveries to our shop.

I always wore this style of clothes, even when we first met. My white long-sleeved blouse, embroidered with red zinnias at the neckline, was scooped in at the waist by my grandmother Carmen's belt and her grandmother's before her. Three petticoats made my outer long skirt swirl when I first danced with Jorge at the winter fair. The key pocket in the belt was only visible to those who could 'see'.

We danced and drank tequila laced with cacao. Many men wanted to dance with me that night, tucking pink roses into my piled-high hair, but it was Jorge I wanted to be with.

Jorge made sure I got home safely that night. The next day he came round with a bunch of roses, and nestled in the central bloom was an engagement ring. I accepted straight away. We married and early the following year Natalia was born.

As I looked down at the soup, a tear splashed into the deep tomato red. Things seemed so perfect then, so full of hope, and now, so many years later, it's hard to believe we lost our little girl.

"Hello, Alma! We're hungry!" The foreman crashed into the kitchen and, without invitation, screeched the wooden dining chair along the terracotta floor, and squashed his big bottom into it. His men took the other chairs. They stank of petrol and tobacco. The white tiles I had painted with lizards, butterflies, and flowers gleamed behind them. They pressed their dirt-stained elbows on the starched cotton tablecloth that I had ironed and pressed.

"You're in my kitchen. Go wash your hands in the sink by the door!" I said.

The foreman spat on his hands and rubbed them together. "That'll do you, lady, now give me my dinner!" A fire of anger rose inside me, and I heaped another spoonful of chili and added it to the bowl of soup I had just poured for him.

"C'mon boss, do as the lady says," said a man, washing his hands.

"My hands are clean enough," said the foreman and started eating.

I continued to ladle the steaming soup into the terracotta bowls, tutting under my breath, and gave each a sprinkle of coriander, with a half-smile, knowing the chili would soon be flowing down the foreman's throat. Jorge was out back cutting more coriander, so thankfully, he didn't see what I had done. He would not have approved. The smell powered me to continue serving a meal to men I did not feel deserved it.

I opened the oven door, and the room swelled with the warmth of freshly baked jalapeño cornbread. All the men looked over as Jorge came back into the kitchen with a basket of herbs and smiled seeing the appreciation of my food: "Ah you like my Alma's food? It makes tired men strong."

My hands wrapped in thick oven mitts pulled out the cast iron skillet, and I smiled seeing the foreman already breaking into a sweat. I set the steaming golden cake in the center and cut it into large chunks with my snake-handled knife. From nowhere I saw my eldest sister Catalina, the family matriarch, pass by the window. She looked at me and frowned.

None of my other nine sisters were with her. Catalina was probably checking on us one by one, making sure that we were doing 'the work' of looking after our motherland in the way passed down to us.

Francisca, my next in line, would be selling herbs and remedies at the market. For sure, Catalina would oversee the addition of any snake oil that she was wont to add. Other sisters would be either shepherding the animals on the hills, tending vegetables, or exercising other gifts.

These men were from the city, disconnected from the land, but eating my food made them reminisce.

"When I was a boy, *mi madre* used to make this," said the man with the red checked shirt.

Another, who I heard them call Antonio, said "Mi padre worked long hours growing corn as tall as two men" So, the conversations went on.

Jorge came in with shots of tequila for them to have with my special cacao and chili truffles. They had wandered into talking about time in the woods and finding wild food.

I smiled. The food was working. Maybe there was no need for me to go. Perhaps I could prevent them from cutting down the forests with my magical cookery. But the foreman got up and slammed his glass on the table. "Back to work!" he ordered.

With reluctance, the men left the table, stacked their dishes, and set them by the sink. All except the foreman raised their caps to me and with their hands over chests gave me a little bow.

Soon the sawing got loud again. I could hear the metal chains creating bondage in the beautiful trees nearby. Caracaras squawked, and there was a tapping on the window. A raven was banging something against the glass. I opened the window, and she dropped the black key onto the windowsill. The bird looked me in the eye, flapped its wings, and flew east up the mountainside. I felt my belt, and the key was no longer in my pocket. I showed Jorge.

"Alma. You must go," Jorge said with wet eyes.

"Jorge, remember to visit me."

"I will, my love. I'll clear up here."

With a tear in my eye, I unhooked my blue and green cape from the back of the door, wrapped it around me, and covered my head with the hood. I climbed the rocks up the mountainside, there would be another four hours before nightfall.

Raven sat high on a tree waiting. Below I could hear the sounds of destruction. Orange and black monarch butterflies circled in frantic flights above the pine and oak trees, looking for a new home. The monkeys shrieked, baring their teeth at the cranes and lorries that swung toward them.

The river flowed with fury, loaded with its tall dead companions whose roots had stopped the riverbanks from bursting. The jaguars, deep in the forest, gnawed on their latest prey, ready to pounce should any of the loggers venture into their lair.

It had been years since I last went home. New orchids sprang amongst the creepers that twisted around the trees. Raven lit her eyes to deep turquoise and shone a path for me to follow. Some rocks had fallen over the track, disturbed by the carnage in the lower ground. The rain began to fall. I climbed over sharp rocks slipping on the wet moss.

Leaning on a wet oak tree, I stopped to free my shoes of debris when a frog leaped out and sky-dived into a turbulent waterfall. I gasped. I reached out, grabbed an overhanging bough, and hauled myself up to a higher rock. I pushed my feet into crevices and used my hands like claws claiming my ascent on anything I could. A long snout came face to face with me. I froze, then sighed with relief seeing Armadillo scuttle away behind boulders. I smiled and with ease climbed still higher, knowing I was surrounded by the wildlife I had grown up with. I mused over all the times I had become them to escape my parents' demands to help the villagers.

My cape caught on a branch. I lost my footing and swung like a suspended bat trying to grab the protruding tree roots. The heavy rains poured into the waterfall that crashed beneath me. Icy spray covered me, as I hooked my foot into a hanging rope vine and then I heard a snarling.

Above me, I could see the silhouette of a black jaguar looming over me. My heartbeat fast. I had had little to eat and had only slept a few hours last night. There was little strength in my arms, and I knew any sudden movement would threaten the jaguar. Raven swooped down, took the key from my belt, and flew past the jaguar who retreated. I heard voices.

"Alma, get hold of this!" Catalina's voice echoed.

"We're here!" Francesca called.

I grasped the rope. A shrill sound pierced my ears, and I found myself catapulted up the hillside. I landed flat on my back. My ten sisters stood in a circle around me.

"What took you so long?" Catalina asked. "We've been waiting for you since dusk."

"The way is not as I remember."

"Ah, you just weren't concentrating." Catalina always riled me up. I gritted my teeth, sat up, and dusted down my sodden cape.

"We know about the extra chili. We told you not to. . ."

Some of my sisters suppressed smiles, but their serious gazes remained fixed on Catalina.

"That foreman will be running to the toilet for the rest of the week!" she said, sternly.

At this, my sisters could hold it no longer, and all exploded in laughter. I joined in, relieved to let out the tension from my near descent into the river.

"Hush!" Catalina said. Everyone quietened. "Alma, open the door."

Raven flew onto my shoulder with the black key in her beak. I took it from her and opened the cave door. The eleven of us and Raven entered. None of us had been there for decades but, like always, the pan steamed over the crackling fire. We each took down our bowls hung around the fireplace, and Catalina filled them with hot broth. One bowl was left hanging.

I woke later as Catalina dragged me across the floor. "Alright, alright," I said. "I'm awake."

"Really?" Catalina asked. "About time."

It irked me that she had never given up what she saw as the mantle of the older sister, even though I had learned much more about medicine than her. and I was the only one who had married.

However, I had not been able to carry the family line into the future. I knew Catalina wanted to ensure the protection of the forest. We were all getting older and now the loggers had moved in. She worried about how to achieve this.

The others sat in a circle, each holding a small crystal. There was one place left for me. I joined them as Raven sat on my shoulder. Catalina placed a larger crystal like an Ostrich egg in the center and surrounded it with candles.

My vision blurred as an image emerged of the forest. The jaguars, high in the trees, clung to the upper branches, and the monkeys swung wildly from tree to tree as the sawing and felling of trees reached a deafening roar.

In the half-light, my sisters' somber faces merged with the forest scene. One looked back at me with golden eyes and a wet black nose and whiskers, another with green eyes and a face covered in leathery scales. Each one appeared to change from animal to human with the flickering candles.

"Pick the berries and make sure you get the deepest purple!" Catalina called.

Each night, after a day of cooking and chanting, we sat together with our crystals and prayed for the forest, but each time we looked into the giant egg crystal there was little change.

Sometimes the loggers looked a little tired and finished early. Although Catalina was annoyed that I had put the foreman out of action for a week, she had to admit that at least without him the loggers' progress at felling trees had slowed.

The more tired Catalina got, the more she ordered us around, complaining that the tea wc brewed her was cold and, the worst insult of all, that we 'had lost focus'.

After much shouting and arguments, she finally said it.

"There is only one option left. Without a descendant, Alma must shift back."

Each sister stepped forward and they hugged me one by one. My face was wet with their tears. Catalina came last. She pulled me close, gave me the sweetest kiss on my head, and placed a gold ring inscribed with ancient text on my index finger.

I held out my hand to touch her, but she turned away. They all left, and Raven flew out with them. I set about making my human offering to heal the forest and packed into a seed pod a hair, a piece of my nail, and spit to seal it. Leaving it on the mantelpiece I knew that my sisters would plant it in the forest and my magic would provide the healing the forest needed.

Later that night there was a knock on the cave door. It was Jorge. He hugged me and told me how everyone was missing my truffles and that the loggers kept coming around asking when I would be home. "But are they still cutting down the forest?" Jorge hung his head low. "More disappears each day."

Raven listened, perched with her head cocked on one side, and knew she had to leave us.

We lay by the fire, embraced one another, and made love. Jorge caressed me in a way I had not known since that night when, so engrossed in one another, we didn't notice Natalia slip downstairs.

Catalina and my older sisters still sat in their circle, morphed into their animal spirits, and sat around us, listening to our ancestors. There was only one way to stop the greed of urban development from eating up the natural world.

Natalia was a small curious child, and unbeknown to them had hidden behind the sofa that day. She did not know how to use magical protection from their incantations. Natalia's small body could only absorb it. At first, they didn't hear her coughing as her human voice left her. It was only when they heard the distinguishable sound of clapping that turned into flapping that they all leapt to find her changed.

Born human, Natalia had no power to shift back. I continued to wear the style of clothes from that night hoping she would return as my little girl.

Jorge kissed my neck, slowly down to my breasts. I responded by touching his thick head of hair, running my fingers down the nape of his neck, and circling his earlobes until we entwined in orgasmic pleasure, no longer two people. We cried out as we left our bodies to be reunited with our daughter. The candles went out.

The next morning the caracaras were singing their song when the foreman marched up the mountainside with his men. He was angry at finding all his machinery inoperable, all shipping and logging on strike, and people protesting against his company's bully tactics on the streets of all major cities.

With Jorge gone as well as me, he suspected. "Search the area and beat the ground, until we find that witch!"

The frightened men trampled over tree roots and slipped over rocks. One fell. Grasping at branches and with rocks crashing below him he tumbled to the ground and his head hit hard against the door of our mountain house. It swung open to reveal the scene of our special reunion the night before.

"Here's Alma's cape!" Antonio called.

Another man ran to join him, picking up the shoes and cap. "Jorge's?"

"What the!?" shouted the foreman, as Raven landed on his bald head and drew blood with her claws.

We three ravens flew over the men.

Horses from the Sky
Ate Her Sugar Lump Eyes

by Zoltán Komor

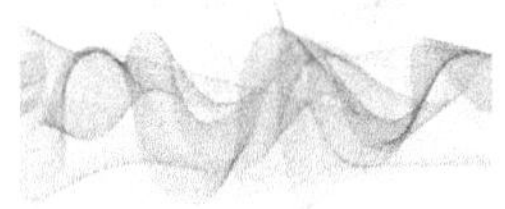

The girl stands at the window with a slingshot in her hand. She scratches out her eyeballs and shoots them into the clouds, yelling, "Go! Go and see the world!"

Her eyes fly over the snowy roofs of the village, where birds stand aside to give them way. Finally, the eyeballs slam into the side of a sauntering cow at the village border. They sink deep under its skin, into its flesh, and a painful moo tears up the grey clouds in the sky.

"What a prisoner I am in this ugly house!" sighs the blind girl, cowering on the ground, hitting the old boards of the wooden floor with her weak little fists, trying to cry without eyes. "This whole village is just a cage. The world just grows and grows outside, while I'm shrinking here."

Hearing the noise, her stooped, old mother steps into the room. When she glimpses the deep, red pits where her daughter's deep blue eyes used to glint, she screams: "Oh, you fool! Your beautiful eyepearls! Come on, stand up, you'll catch pneumonia down there! Lizards will build a nest into your throat, I tell you!"

"Enough, Mother! Stop telling me what to do!" mutters the girl, but she's too weak to resist. Soon, her father arrives too and puts her in bed, blanketing her.

"Stay there, young lady!" groans her dad. "You know you are such a weak little child, if you would go to the kitchen, the spoons would crawl under your skin! If you would step onto the doorsill, maggots would bite into your toenails! Ugly germs lurk in this world, and even dewy air can destroy your beautiful paper skin!"

"My weakness exists only in your head!" answers the girl, but they cook a soup from the potty, and the hot liquid seals her mouth.

It's afternoon. The family is pouring coffee, boiled from black flies into small cups. When they throw the sugar cubes into the streaming drink, the father recognizes his daughter's sweet look in one of the lumps.

It gives him an idea.

He steps to his daughter's bed and drops sugar cubes into the girl's empty red eye sockets one into each.

"Now look at that! My daughter is so beauteous!" He cheers, pointing at the girl's new sugar eyes. She just blinks and blinks, but still, she can only see the moving insides of a cow.

"If I could, I would put her into a showcase and just gaze at her from dawn to dusk. Of course, now and then, I would wipe the spider webs off of her, but that's all. The prettiest birds need to be secured in a cage!"

Night falls. Bad luck oozes out from the horseshoes. The father lies in his bed, and his long beard floats around his face as he snores. In his forehead, like a tiny ballerina, spins his shrunken, two-inch-long daughter. Her toes nearly touch the wrinkled, old skin. It's like she's floating between her father's closed eyes. The sugar cubes are shining in her eye sockets.

"Oh, Father, dear Father!" moans the girl. "I have begged and begged for that ugly cow to give me back my eyes or just puke them out and kick them far away, but it's such an evil and witless animal! At daylight, I almost accept my cage, but at nighttime, Father, I would bite your throats, and bathe in your blood! Doesn't every animal feel the same about their keepers? All birds hate fowlers."

Her sugar eyes cry sweet honey onto her father's mouth. She just cries and cries, until the man can't swallow anymore, and he begins to choke from the golden liquid.

"Father . . . oh, Father . . ." cries the girl. The old man squirms in his bed, rumpling the sheets with his kicking legs. Then he dies. A wind arrives, picking up the girl. It carries her and puts her down onto her mother's forehead and soon the honey fills her mouth too.

Door handles made of dead bees; rotting feathers in the pillow; somewhere in the night a long sausage, like a deadly snake, coils around a steak hammer. The blind girl keeps prodding the walls, and soon, she finds the door. Crawling outside into the freezing night, she leaves her footsteps in the snow.

"How sweet is the air, how big is the world!" she yells. Her long, blonde hair reaches up and tickles the clouds' bellies. The sky laughs up two flying horses, which begin to chase the girl from above.

"Look, what an ugly pale mole crawled out from her hole!" neighs one of them.

"Don't be so rude, Freckles, look, she brought us presents!" They slope downward and kick the blind girl with their hooves. She falls onto her back.

"Bon à petite!" whinnies Freckles, biting out one of the sugar cubes from the screaming girl's face.

"The Lord's supper can't be better!" says the other as the sugar crackles between its teeth.

"Such a sweet girl, I hope she doesn't catch a cold!" laughs Freckles, coughing dark worms into her face.

"A little chill never killed anyone!" says the other. Then they spring into the air and disappear into the sky.

"Oh, Father. Oh, Mother," stutters the girl, watching the insides of the sleeping cow, trying to read out her fortune. "The ugly germs found me like you always said they would. My throat. . . It hurts. And fever has set my thoughts on fire. I wish I had just stayed in my room. I wish you were here to take care of me. . ."

The girl doesn't stand up; she just lies there, as if she were in her comfy little bed. The snow begins to fall. Soon, a cold blanket grows around her body.

When morning arrives, she's just a bulge, a puckering on the white canvas. Her eyes inside of the cow are not glinting anymore; they are motionless marbles. The cowbell rings sadly on the animal's neck as though it wants to call the villagers together for a funeral. But no one comes; everyone stays inside their warm homes.

In the sky, the old boards of Heaven's wooden floor crack, as a ghost keeps knocking on it from beneath, with its weak little fists.

On a Midwinter's Eve

by Vonnie Winslow Crist

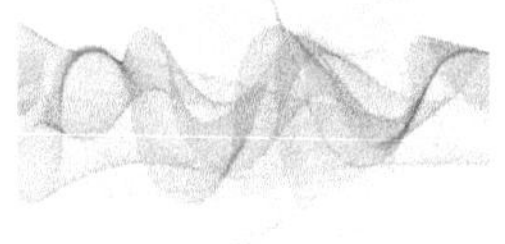

Beneath the scant shelter of a spruce, Brock paused and wiped snow from his eyes, cheeks, nose, and mouth. The weather had taken a dangerous turn not long after he'd departed the cabin, and he now found himself calf-deep in drifts with no dinner bagged. *Bagged?* He snorted out a cloud of warm breath as he resumed his search for a deer. He had brought no bag. Anything he managed to shoot would have to be carried on his broad back or flung on a pine bough and dragged home.

And why the sudden longing for venison? He had rarely hunted with anything more deadly than a camera these past five years. He was, after all, a researcher paid by others to find background information for magazine articles, books, genealogy projects, and such who had grown to love a comfortable apartment life.

In fact, it was a fluke that he was even at the cabin. After his dad's death earlier this month, Brock had decided to move his computer, work files, book collection, and other belongings to the log structure. He had inherited the building and the land it stood on, free and clear, so he was saving a wad of cash by staying here. And he had all he needed: internet access, mail delivery, electricity, indoor plumbing, a working well, phone service, and a store not too far away.

But ever since he had heard the persistent calls of a barn owl last night, the well-stocked pantry and full freezer seemed inadequate. He could think of nothing but deer meat. And when he thought of the smell of venison roasting over the fire, he actually found his mouth filled with saliva.

Therefore, after this morning's coffee and oatmeal, he had hauled several loads of firewood from the shed to the cabin's porch, double-checked the supply of kerosene for the emergency lanterns, and unpacked a couple of extra blankets from the cedar chest. He knew the telephone and electric lines strung up the mountainside from the road might be damaged by the weight of the predicted ice and snow and wanted to be ready just in case. When the storm preparations were completed, he had searched through the contents of the attic and located his old crossbow.

He looked at the bow in his right hand. A gift from his father, Brock had used it to take the life of at least a dozen bucks over the years. He shivered and pulled his knit cap down lower on his head. He did not like to think of those venison steaks and burgers as a former deer. It was easier to think of them as meat that arrived packaged and labeled from the butcher's shop.

To his left, Brock heard branches breaking. He froze. He needed to stop musing over past hunts and focus on the task ahead. With eyes narrowed, he scrutinized the swath of forest where he thought the snaps had emanated from: tree trunks, boulders, snowdrifts, debris, and a bit of brown fur visible beneath the drooping branches of an evergreen tree.

Fur! Arrow notched and ready, Brock raised his bow in slow motion. Determined to be as stealthy as a fox, his shallow breaths seemed to shatter the quiet. Just as his finger began to squeeze the trigger, a pale owl dropped from a branch above him and snatched the wool cap from his head.

Surprised, he yelped and swatted at the creature. Then, afraid the bird might return to grab more than a knit hat, Brock lowered his bow, crouched down, and searched the gray skies for the owl.

It was not long before he spotted the thief. It was perched on a gnarled oak branch, glaring at him.

"What's it to you?" he called to the bird.

He was not worried about frightening away the game. Any respectable deer would have bolted at his first surprised shout.

"It was bigger than a mouse. And I am just as hungry as you are."

"Kschh! Kschh! Kschh!" responded the owl.

Brock would have felt better if the creature had hooted at him. The owl's eerie rasping hiss combined with its dark eyes boring into his eyes made his heart pound. He recognized the bird as a barn owl by its heart-shaped face. Perhaps it was the same creature that called outside his window last night. But why would it follow him into the forest? And where was its nest? He had been spending time at the cabin since boyhood and knew of no barns or other buildings this deep in the woods.

"And where is your home? I might need it if this storm continues."

Again, the owl hissed, "Kschh! Kschh! Kschh!"

"You are useless. I cannot understand a word of your chatter. So, go your way, and leave me to my hunt. That deer can't have gotten too far."

"Then, can you understand me, Hunter?" said an elderly woman garbed in a tattered robe as she stepped from behind the evergreen with the sagging branches.

Brock gaped at the woman. Below her hood, her face had turned blue from the bitter winds and freezing temperatures. It was the most severe case of frostbite he had ever seen.

"Ma'am, we need to find you shelter. See if we can warm you up." He glanced down at her bony fingers protruding from ragged sleeves. They were even bluer than her face. "And I don't think there is any time to lose."

The woman cackled. "I would be more concerned about your safety than mine." Then, she gestured with her staff towards a rock outcrop. "There is a cave over there."

For a split second, Brock felt the urge to flee in the opposite direction of the old woman's cave, but the howling of the wind had increased to blizzard levels. Any shelter at this point would be better than staying out in the elements, besides the woman obviously needed whatever first aid he could render. And so, he followed her, slogging his way through the drifts, and hoping there was a spot to build a fire inside the cave.

"In here, Hunter," said the elderly woman as she ducked under a low shelf of rock and vanished into an opening between two boulders.

Brock followed. After traversing a narrow passageway, he found himself in a large room brightly lit by lanterns and candles. There was a fire crackling on a stone hearth at one end, two wide wooden benches covered with blankets and pillows at the other, and a table and several crude chairs in the middle of the room. The cantankerous barn owl was comfortably roosted on one of the chair backs still clutching Brock's knit cap in its talons.

"I would like that returned," he said and took several steps toward the bird.

"Kschh! Kschh! Kschh!" The owl tilted its head and appeared to laugh at him. Next, the bird used its hooked bill to pull a thread out of the cap. It paused, and eyed Brock.

"Apologize, and he might give it back," suggested the blue-faced woman.

"Apologize!" Brock glanced at the barn owl. The bird tugged the thread again, looked in his direction, and opened its beak.

"Okay. I am sorry I was trying to shoot your deer friend for my dinner. Can I have my hat back?"

The owl lifted, flew to Brock, and tossed the cap into his hands. As the bird returned to the chair back, Brock noticed its legs were long and its wing feathers were tawny with a few cinnamon and gray patches on them. The bird's fluttery wing-strokes reminded him of a pale summer moth, even though it was the dead of winter.

"Thanks."

The owl nodded.

Suddenly, Brock remembered the frostbitten woman. He shifted his gaze to her, only to find she was studying him with pursed blue-black lips. "What foolishness sent you out on winter solstice at owl-light?"

"Owl-light?"

"Twilight, then," said the crone as she removed her robe and tossed it on one of the benches.

The long ice-blue sweater and bluish-white dress she wore beneath the robe were worn and oft-patched. On her feet, she wore heavy black boots, and around her neck draped a necklace with a large colorless stone dangling from its center. Her hair was twined in a long gray braid and her eyes were black—so black, it seemed to Brock that they were all pupils.

But it was her blue skin that shocked him. That was until he recalled reading about a man from the western part of the United States who ate a little bit of silver every day in the belief it made him healthier. He had turned blue. Granted it was a grayer blue than the woman before him, but the man had turned a shade of blue because of silver consumption. Since the woman's blueness did not seem to be causing her pain, Brock supposed the old lady had also ingested silver over a long period of time.

"Call-yak," said the blue-faced woman as she went to the fire, lifted the lid of a black pot, and stirred its contents.

"Excuse me?"

"You may call me Call-yak. Would you like a plate of stew in lieu of a deer?"

"Well. . ." Brock rubbed his chin. To take food from a stranger was not something he would usually consider, but he was famished. If he did not know better, he would have thought there was a tapeworm gnawing away inside his belly. He studied the woman's face again. She seemed a little younger and a little less blue.

"Yes. That is, if it is not too much trouble. I could use a plate of stew. And my name is Brock. I am sorry if I was rude just now, but–"

"The skin color surprised you." Call-yak finished his sentence. "Few people know what to expect when the moon is waning and the North Wind howls like a wolf."

The word *wolf* had barely been uttered when a white wolf padded into the room, calmly looked at Brock, and went and curled up by the fire. Call-yak glanced at the wolf, smiled, and handed Brock a plate of stew and a spoon.

Brock backed to one of the chairs, pulled it out, sat down opposite the barn owl, and dipped the utensil into the thick stew. He wondered again if it was safe to eat and delayed actually tasting the concoction by stirring and blowing across its surface.

Call-yak dished out a second plate of stew and placed it between the paws of the wolf. The great beast gave Brock a look of disdain and proceeded to gulp down the vegetable mixture.

"Is the stew not to your liking?"

There was a challenge in Call-yak's voice. A voice, Brock noticed, that was less filled with the rasp of old age than a moment earlier.

"Would you rather have deer?" she queried.

As she said the word *deer*, three does strolled into the room, trotted over to the blanket-draped benches, and knelt. The three bowed their heads to Call-yak, then lay like obedient dogs beside the sleeping benches.

The owl, who had managed to keep his thoughts to himself until now, chortled, "Kschh! Kschh! Kschh!" Which now sounded to Brock quite like, "Witch, witch, witch!"

Seeing no out, Brock ate a spoonful of Call-yak's stew. It was more delicious than anything he had ever eaten. While savory, there was an unmistakable sweetness to it that summoned memories of roasted onions, sweet potatoes, apples, and carrots. Its thick gravy coated his tongue with what he assumed was fat. But fat from what? As for the herbs and spices, they reminded him of long-ago holiday feasts with his grandparents. Though unable to identify the contents of Call-yak's stew, nevertheless he gobbled it up. But Brock felt more ravenous than before.

"More?" asked the blue-faced woman as she ladled out another serving of stew with hands now smooth and young-looking. And it seemed to Brock that her clothing was not quite as tattered as he had first thought.

Again, Brock cleaned his plate. As he finished the last spoonful of the vegetable stew, he realized that Call-yak's braided hair was now as black as her eyes and her ice-blue gown and sweater now flowed around a younger, curvier body. He squinted. The blue-faced woman's skin was wrinkle-free, and her lips seemed fuller and strangely seductive.

He agreed to another refill. The barn owl flew over to the table and stood by Brock's plate. The owl raised and lowered its head with every mouthful he consumed. And its eyes seemed bright with intelligence. He turned to make a comment to

Call-yak about the sentient owl but found himself unable to speak.

Call-yak's ebony hair tumbled down her back and around her shoulders. Three braided silver chains with blue and clear jewels attached crossed her brow and wrapped around her head like a delicate crown. At regular intervals, long strands of silver chains bejeweled with the same blue and clear crystals dangled among the locks of her hair.

"More?" asked the stunningly beautiful Call-yak.

He nodded and held out his plate for a refill. After the fourth plateful of vegetable stew, his belt felt too tight. Brock loosened the offending leather strap and buckle and gazed longingly at the black kettle. He was a big man, solid and muscular, but another helping of dinner would never stay down.

"A glass of milk to top it off?" Call-yak's melodic voice encouraged, as she poured milk from a pottery pitcher into a mug. Brock saw there was snow still clinging to the outside of the pitcher.

"That sounds perfect," he replied as he grasped the mug's handle and drank the chilly liquid. "I do not believe I have ever tasted better milk," he began. "I guess it is because. . ."

"It is deer milk," finished the woman whose headdress now included a cluster of white feathers on either side of her head. "For the deer are my cattle, the wolves are my dogs, and this owl is my dearest friend."

Too full to stand, Brock merely raised his arms, then let them fall into his lap. "I did not know. Honestly, I meant no offense it's just that I was–"

"Hungry?" Call-yak laced her delicate blue fingers together. "Are you hungry now?"

"No, but. . ."

"No." The enchanting maiden with the pale skin, tinted ever so faintly blue, strolled over, leaned down, stared into Brock's brown eyes with her black pupils. "From this day forward, you will never taste animal flesh. Should you put so much as a crumb of meat into your mouth, you will change into your namesake."

"I don't understand."

"Brock," stated the woman, "is the Old Ones' name for a badger."

"Badger!"

"Indeed." The woman used a fingernail to trace a symbol on his forehead. Before he dared ask what she was doing, Call-yak explained, "Rune. I have traced a binding rune upon you, Brock, Badger of a Man. Henceforth, you are a friend and protector of animals and a servant of Cailleac Bhuer."

"Who is–"

"Call-y'ac V'fhoor?" the woman said with a twisted smile. "'Tis I, Daughter of the Winter Sun, Ancient Fairy of Midwinter, Protector of Deer and Wolves. Some call me Blue Hag, some Stone Woman, some Goddess. I am all of those things, and none of them."

Brock frowned. "Was the old woman from the forest your true form? Or is the young-looking woman before me now, really you?"

Call-yak laughed, a lovely laugh that sounded like small birds singing and the ice-encrusted branches of a fir tree tapping together. "Neither Badger-Man. They are both glamour."

The fairy cupped his chin in her cold blue hands. "And would you stay with me if I were the beauty before you?"

He did not know how to respond. A part of him wanted to nod his head and stay with the Protector of Deer and Wolves. But another part of Brock wondered what sort of creature was hidden by the glamour.

The Ancient Fairy of Midwinter smiled. "Someday, Badger-Man, you will indeed see my true form, but not today." Then, she clutched the crystal orb hanging on her necklace, and continued, "You have eaten fairy food and will crave it always, but do not search for this cave."

Before Brock could respond Call-yak snapped her fingers and the pale owl flew to her shoulder. She whispered something to the bird, and it clicked its beak in response. She snapped her fingers again, and Brock finally felt himself able to stand.

He rose slowly, a little unsteady on his feet. A sudden thought crossed his mind. He had spent time in a fairy cave, and legend said that time flowed at a different speed in Faerie.

"How much time have I lost?"

"Not long," answered Call-yak of the pale skin, dark hair, and a snowy gown.

"Will the world have changed so much I cannot recognize it?" Brock asked. He was afraid of the answer.

The fairy shook her head. "Only a week has passed outside this cave, and badgers are fond of spending much of the winter underground."

Brock ignored the badger comment. "Thank you for your hospitality, Call-yak," he said as he edged towards the cave entrance.

"It is because of your lack of aggression towards my owl and your concern for my imagined frostbite that I showed you hospitality. But tread carefully, Badger Man. Next time, I might not be in such an amicable mood."

The wolf trotted over and stood to the left of the beautiful fairy. The deer rose, clip-clopped to the right-hand side of the Daughter of the Winter Sun.

"My owl will lead you to your cabin. Keep your eyes on him and do not look back. A single glance over your shoulder, or a single word to anyone of what has transpired here, or a single bite of animal flesh, and you will find yourself on all fours wandering through the world in badger form."

"You have my word that I won't–"

"I do not need your word," responded the Daughter of the Winter Sun. "A deal has been struck, and my spells are strong."

Brock pulled his slightly damaged knit cap on his head as he took another step in the direction of the entrance. "Will I see you again?"

The blue-faced woman shrugged her shoulders. "My friends will watch you always, and I will peer through the trees in your direction whenever the North Wind blusters and snows fall at midwinter." Then, she added as the owl flew from her shoulder, "Especially if the moon is waning, and it is owl-light."

As instructed, Brock kept his eyes on the barn owl as it flapped out of the cave into the predawn twilight. He thought he heard the

Daughter of the Winter Sun, Ancient Fairy of Midwinter, and Protector of Deer and Wolves call, "Fare-thee-well, Badger Man," as he neared the edge of the forest, but he dared not respond.

And when he saw his cabin in the distance, Brock was acutely aware of four things: the eerie, "Kschh! Kschh! Kschh!" of the ghostly owl overhead, the heaviness of his bow, the eyes of hundreds of woodland animals locked upon him, and a terrible longing to return to the cave of Call-yak.

Mortal Wound

by Ross Jeffery

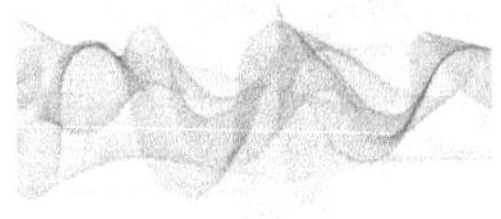

The cedar tree where we first kissed stands before me. I don't know why I've come here; all it houses are memories I'd do best to forget.

Its limbs spread heavenward, layer upon layer, the perfect visual expression of a family tree. Wider at the bottom where we'd belong, I glance up as it grows taller and thinner, reaching to the blue sky where our ancient ancestors sit in the heavens at the top looking down on us with scorn.

The sun's out and a light sweat dampens my underarms, a slight trickle of moisture snakes its way down my back, my shirt sticking to my flesh in all the wrong places. It's claustrophobic and feels as if clammy hands are smothering me, which is an odd sensation given the open fields that abound. It's in this moment that my thoughts turn back to you and the cruel work of your hands on my flesh.

I observe each layer of the tree as I approach, each adding to the next in a canopy of interconnectedness and I realize that's why I've come, to feel closer to you in your absence. Even though you're gone I can't escape your presence as it appears in the life around me.

Even in death, your little atrocities remain.

I shuffle under the sagging green limbs that hang low, worn down by time or is it the memories of us being here that wilt the branches, as the roots of the tree drink up our failures? I know first-hand how oppressive the weight of failure can be, and it's taken me a long time to stand straight, to hold my head high, but I'm getting used to this new view, day by day, week by week, year by year.

Within this space I feel safe, I feel as though the branches reach down to embrace me, to hold me close and protect me – as the wind moves through its branches I hear the tree sigh, it feels sorry for me in a way. It's as if this testament to patience and time of growth and renewal has witnessed the slow withering of me under your ever-present shade. I press forward and walk to the trunk that bears witness to us. Etched deep within its bark is our declaration of love, a scar on the world.

I press my fingers to the wound and the tips of my fingers trace over the rough darkened etching *TC **and** JP **forever***.

The sudden memories hurt and so I glance away. I stand at the foot of the tree and stare into the canopy above. I'm struck by the warmth of the sun that dapples my flesh as if I'm being kissed for the first time.

With my fingers still tracing the declaration of our love from so long ago, I realize that in a strange way, I am part of something bigger and I feel overwhelmed at the sight of this titan of the forest before me, the one that we marred with our love. It hasn't succumbed to the wounds of us that mar its flesh, but it in turn shows that to persevere is to flourish and that through it all we can survive, and I guess that's what I am really, a survivor. You see the rings of a tree stump denote the passage of time and circumstance.

I have my own rings, buried beneath the surface of my skin, the aged bruises that used to circle my arms and legs would denote the passage of my own life, my own circumstances, but you can't see them for looking at me, buried below the surface, mottled and faded. I guess my flesh is now free. Free of him.

I turn, place my back against the tree, and feel the bark bite at my back as I slide down to sit on the ground. It's nice to feel something other than your fists finding my flesh and the fear that clung to me like a second skin. I sit, my mind turning to all the times we came here, to our Cedar tree.

The Seventh Kiss

We first met under this tree many years ago now. We were said to be young love's dream. It was before things turned sour, before the words of your lips could wind me and strip me of my dignity. Your words were a poison that had no antidote. They caused me to lose sight of who I was and what I could be. You clipped my wings and kept me grounded. Your words raped me of everything I knew. They cut deep and true. You removed my support, and you chipped away at my foundations until I couldn't live without your scaffolding to hold me up. Because if you left, I'd quite literally fall apart, crumbling to dust in your absence.

When you hear the same thing repeated again and again you start to believe it–I was no good, a tramp, a busy body, a useless cook, a prick tease, and a slovenly slut. I was an unfit mother, a lay about, an ungrateful bitch, a selfish cow, and an ugly fat pig.

There was no me anymore, there was only us, because to remove myself from you was to commit suicide, because as you said often "Who would have me?"

I had no one, and you knew that. You kept me on a tight leash, made me quit my job, and alienated me from friends and family by ensuring I was kept busy playing housewife. You bought me drab clothes to stop wandering eyes from finding me, and you decided when I could drink or eat and how much and at what time. Then you quickly cut my rations when you thought I had got too fat sitting around the house, which I never did, but you felt that I needed correcting for. I somehow let you ruin me over time, and you made me believe that I deserved that ruin.

Today's kiss was different from the others, there's a first time for everything I guess. Today you didn't kiss me with your mouth but decided to kiss me with the sharp bones of your knuckles. They quickly found the plumpness of my face and then the roundness of my belly, which doubled me over and sent me crumbling to the floor with all the air driven from my lungs. I choked on the ground and while I was down there you kissed me again but this time with the toe of your boot, again and again, you found ways of showing me how much you cared. But not once did you kiss me with your lips. Our declaration of love was carved on the trunk above you, a taunting whisper from the past.

The Fifth Kiss

This was when you truly meant it; you kissed me lovingly, hopefully, and with tears slicking our faces together. You'd told me that it wasn't my fault, and I believed you. That passion filled kiss, it's what kept me hanging on, hoping that you'd actually changed and hope reigned albeit fleetingly and I craved it more than life itself.

A week before this kiss I'd fallen over in the street. I was grocery shopping which was one of the only times you'd allow me out without you as a chaperone. When I tripped on a paving slab the bags I carried scattered around me. Fruit and vegetables, tins of food, and bottles of beer rolled down the street and into the gutter. I'd gone down hard, hit my stomach on the unyielding pavement. Little did I know then that the pavement didn't hit as hard as your fists.

I was helped to my feet by an elderly man. As his hands touched my flesh I felt the warmth of a caring embrace, and it felt electric. Whenever you touched me it was always cold and devoid of love. The man helped me to my feet before he left me to inspect my wounds.

He was down on his knees in moments, every inch the perfect gentleman, he began to collect my shopping from the road, gutter, and pavement. Turning back to me the man froze.

He was still crouched, he was staring at me strangely, he wasn't even looking at my face, he was staring lower, much lower than any gentleman should.

It was then I felt something trickle warmly from between my legs. I realized in that moment that the life I was carrying, the son who'd grow up to be just like his daddy was leaving me in a warm bloody trickle down my leg. God forgive me, but at that moment, I felt pleased. Pleased that he wouldn't grow up under your tyrannical rule, that you wouldn't be able to bend and mold him to your ways as you had with me. I felt like a monster for thinking that the loss of an innocent life was a blessing. I cried with abandon, but the tears that ran down my face were not for the admission of me being a monster, but instead they were tears of joy.

The Third Kiss

This was the kiss you gave the day your hands found my flesh for the first time. Purple welts ringed my neck, caused by hungry fingers that wanted to squeeze the life out of me, and they almost did until you realized what you were doing.

But if I'm honest I knew that the beast you hid so well was to make more appearances, the veil could only last for so long. How long would it be until you truly hurt me or hit me? But as you said so poignantly *it was all my fault*, that my lack of love for you had driven you into the arms of another woman, again.

In your outburst you claimed that it was my inability to give you the son you so desperately craved that drove you into the arms of another woman, it was *my* fault for your infidelity. And the thing is, I believed you. I could see your reasoning and maybe it's true, maybe I was the person who pushed you away to find love with another, maybe my womb was a hostile place to raise a child. Maybe my churning thoughts of bringing another you into this world had polluted the very soil in which our baby would grow. I should have left then, I should have got out while I could, but you pleaded with me to stay after you removed your hands from my throat. The fear in your eyes at the work of your hands was convincing enough to make me stay.

Your embrace felt like a bear trap, and I was the unfortunate soul trapped within its bite. If I struggled to get away, I'd be injured, and you'd find me as I limped away. You'd find me and put me out of my misery, and you'd quite possibly kill me. So, I stayed.

The Second Kiss

This was the most sorrow filled kiss of the lot. It's the one I still have nightmares about because I chose to stay and fight, but what I didn't know at the time was that in choosing to stay I'd already given up any semblance of the fight I had left. I just didn't know what I know now.

You said you were sorry for fucking that woman, and I believed you.

Promises poured from your mouth like a soothing balm, an anesthetic to my flesh and resolve. I should have run, I should have fled but you begged me to stay, and I in my youth and naivety thought I could change you. Make you a better man, but what I didn't know then is that your words were snake venom, slowly destroying me from within, tenderizing the flesh deep inside of me, cracking my bones, and killing my hope. I can see clearly now what you were then. You were my personal Judas who would betray me kiss after kiss, and I would let you. I somehow gave you permission to destroy me from that day on, how foolish I was to stay.

The First Kiss Under the Cedar Tree

I gave myself to you wholly in the moment we carved our love into the cedar tree. I watched on as the slivers of bark fell to the ground and our promises to one another were finally etched into the place we called ours. I'd heard all about your reputation, but I loved you. Those warnings were just words and opinions, I knew you, the others just saw you. I also in some way reveled in the thrill of disappointing my parents, their anger at our communion thrust me into your waiting arms. You were my poisoned fruit, and I wanted to savor every inch of you.

You promised me your never-ending love and life to its fullest. You pledged yourself to me with words and affirmations, with actions and gifts, and that first sweet kiss.

That first kiss under the cedar tree sealed my love for you and it also sealed my fate.

As I rise from the ground, my thoughts of you tumble away. I step out from the tree and head toward home.

You see I can stand now; I can move without your shadow looming over me because I became a phoenix overnight. I rose from the ashes of my previous life. I shed the skin of the beaten and oppressed on the kitchen floor. I emerged from my battered and bruised husk a changed being that decided I would no longer be marred by your hands, belittled by your words, owned by your tyrannical rule. I would no longer flinch when you came close, cower when you shouted, flee in fear – or cry when you forced yourself upon me.

I can do all this now because I decided to thrust the knife again and again. I fiercely hacked and slashed to sever all the ties that bound me to you, with each swipe I felt liberated, and with each slice, I could feel hope blossom from the wounds I inflicted on you.

I stared down at your corpse – I had survived, I am a survivor.

As I make my way from our tree, I glance back one last time, because I know I will not return.

The knife I'd used to cut you from my life sticks proudly from between our stains on this life.

An Uneasy Paradise

by D. A. D'Amico

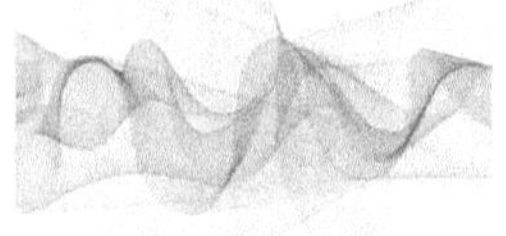

Aishwarya-nau unlocked her main drive sphere as her sisters glided across the pale silver sand. Their polished casings reflected the cinnabar brilliance of the setting sun, throwing ghostly shadows over the meticulously sculpted dunes and out over the craggy basalt ledge.

"It calls." Aishwarya-tihattar rolled to the edge of the grassy path, swiveling to align with the others. "The Core beckons."

Millennia of self-reliance couldn't erase the constraint of programming. Aishwarya spun forward, the summons from the Core undeniable. It was finally time for an accounting.

She veered, halting at the edge of the molded dunes. A dozen of her sisters glided past along the shoreline, their passage leaving parallel streaks on the beach. Erosion and the tide would eventually wash those trails away, but perfection had been ordered, and nothing less would do.

"Divya-satra and Divya-sau." Aishwarya swiveled on her delicate composite base, faceted lenses adjusting to track the hovering ribbons of her companion drones. "Correct this before I return."

The drones collapsed into flattened oval shapes, dropping onto the dunes.

The Earth had been remade in the centuries since humanity had submerged themselves in immense chambers beneath the poles. They'd left one directive: Restore a polluted and overused planet. Make it perfect.

Now, that work was nearly complete.

"Reports from your sisters would indicate our mission has come to an end." The Core flowed in a cascade of pure white light from a carefully sculpted crevasse in the valley's pillar stone, its voice a harmonic synthasia of sound and illumination.

"So very nearly, yes." Aishwarya swiveled to avoid a line of ant-like construction bots. "But . . ."

Rust-infused stalactites hung like bloody teeth, their shadows serrating the jaundiced light from massive arcs set in the chamber roof. Echoes of activity mixed with squeals of worn machinery. Devices of all types scurried through rusting metal conduits, repairing the aged storage vessels, awaiting the release of humanity.

"The others are long finished." If the Core were human, its tone would have held impatience. "You, Aishwarya-nau, are the only unit still in the field. What is your delay?"

Aishwarya rolled back along the chipped granite road, her drive sphere flattening tiny pebbles into dust. She'd been secretly experiencing a logic problem that would've crippled a lesser machine. Her programming demanded perfection, but rationality suggested it could never be possible.

"It's just . . ." she hesitated. "The humans, they made such a mess of the world the first time. I think it's already perfect without them."

She swiveled to track an irregular flake of rust falling from the cavern roof. If this had been Earth's surface, she'd have intercepted the mote long before it hit the ground. "It's peaceful now."

"Humanity is the engine that drives our cause." The Core coalesced, becoming a sphere of ultraviolet brilliance. "End this standoff. Release your masters."

Aishwarya-nau directed eight hundred and six of her Divya drones as they peeled and sanded the bark of trees in a rainbow eucalyptus forest, trying to bring order to unyielding chaotic beauty.

She'd done a great deal of work in the days since her confrontation with the Core but had come no closer to perfection.

"The Core tells me you're dissatisfied."

Aishwarya whirled. If she were human, she'd have been shocked to see the dark man standing beside an unfamiliar vehicle.

"I must complete my programming." Aishwarya spun back to her task.

"Your programming *is* complete." The man stepped around her, his shoes leaving dents on the soft forest floor. "The world is safe again. It's beautiful."

"Safe is not good enough." Aishwarya rolled out of his path, pirouetting to face him once again. Her drive sphere locked, and she trained her sensors on the man.

"Do you know who I am?"

"Only one human may be revived in the event of an emergency." Her sub-processors tracked the Divya drones as she spoke, relaying orders and keeping a real-time watch on their progress. "You are the Guardian."

The man leaned against a tree; his arms folded across his chest. "I am the Guardian, yes."

"I must complete my task." She waited, her chassis at rest. A leaf cascaded slowly by, intercepted by a Divya drone before it could reach the ground. The Guardian sighed.

"It's time to retire, Aishwarya-nau." He leaned forward, staring into her primary lens array. "I'm asking you to return to your cradle and set my people free."

"I cannot."

His steady gaze kept her stationary. Aishwarya desperately wanted to continue her work, but was as helpless as a trained dog in the presence of the Guardian.

"I could make you obey. I could reprogram you." He folded his hands. His voice held none of the tension and cadence of a threat. It registered more melancholy than antagonistic, as if he'd exhausted himself with the chores of his office.

Aishwarya studied the wrinkles on his dark flesh, whorls, and patterns reminiscent of the landscape she hoped to tame. She had no experience outside the mission she'd been created to complete, and she did not want to surrender. She couldn't imagine a time after her usefulness ended.

"When the world is perfect, will I cease to exist?"

The Guardian's head jerked, his eyes wide. "You're *afraid*?"

Aishwarya remained motionless.

"Yes."

The Core erupted in a splash of emerald against the opposing ochre of rust and decay in the immense subterranean chamber. Gigantic cylindrical arcs threw dirty light against the patched and rotting walls. The Guardian stood in the center of the Core's swirling embers, his eyes closed, his expression blank and unreadable.

Aishwarya did not move. She remained where the Guardian had ordered her, but her thoughts were on the surface where her Divya drones continued their futile progress.

She *was* afraid. She hadn't realized it, but the concept of . . . dying took up considerable space in her running processes. She'd never really considered her existence before and had no data on which to rely, but she feared her ending.

"The Core tells me you've become self-aware." The Guardian opened his eyes. Beside him, the Core coalesced into a radiant bar of liquid platinum, inscrutable in its symmetry. "You're alive."

"Then I may continue my task?"

"No."

Aishwarya rolled back, putting distance between herself and the Guardian. The man appeared immensely sad, as if the burden of being humanity's spokesman had worn him down as surely as time, and the elements had worn the supports of the immense storage chamber.

"Will you reprogram me?" If Aishwarya could breathe she'd have held her breath.

"You're no longer fully a machine, and it wouldn't be right to tamper with your . . . life." The Guardian sat on a protruding spur of the chamber's pivot stone.

"You must return to your cradle, Aishwarya-nau." The Core extruded its voice as a staccato blast of pheromones overburdened with a scent reminiscent of cherry blossom and mint.

"If I do not. . ."

"Humanity remains in hibernation." The Guardian stood, pacing the crumbling basalt floor.

Aishwarya struggled with a hesitating drive sphere as she kept pace with the Guardian, mimicking his movements in an attempt to clear her thoughts. She was alive. She understood the implications and wished to continue living. She also now fully understood her desire to exist conflicted with her original programming.

"I do not know how to correct this. . ." Aishwarya spun as a flake of granite as large as a drone slammed into the road in front of her. Others followed in a shower of debris.

She joined the Core as they protected the Guardian, ushering him to a structurally secure part of the chamber, while at the same time issuing instructions to repair bots and coordinating the arrival of Divya's from the surface to shore up the eroding structure.

"Thank you." The Guardian, panting and pale, rested in an arched alcove of the main chamber. His fingers shook as he brushed a stray lock of dust-covered hair from his eyes.

Aishwarya-nau rolled close, her thoughts as jumbled as the heaps of ancient machinery around her. The collapse had given her an idea. "I cannot surrender my life. . ."

"I would never force you to."

"But if you set me another task, I would be able to release my prime objective." If she were human, she would have smiled.

The Guardian stared at her with a strange expression on his trim features, and then he too smiled as he grasped her intent. "What are you asking? Name it, and it's yours if it means freeing mankind."

"Set me another task." She warbled, the sensation of satisfaction blossoming in her process tree as the conflict dwindled. "Give me a different world. Give me *this* underground world, and I will make it perfect."

The Guardian smiled. "How about we settle for something slightly less than perfect this time?"

Bittersweet

by D.A. D'Amico

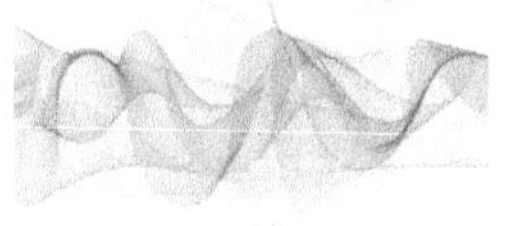

The first shot grazed the cup. It sliced through the marshmallow topping, ripping into the plastic Santa behind. Tinsel flew everywhere. I dived to cover the cocoa, snatching a plastic lid from the floor as I slid behind the beige linoleum counter.

"Hold up!" I screamed, more from the scalding liquid than the bullets whizzing overhead. "I'm human! Stop shooting already!"

My mouth watered. The aroma of fine Dutch chocolate wafted through the steam.

"Is it safe?" The voice, tense, feminine, echoed through the empty cafe. "Tell me you didn't spill it."

"I'm okay, thanks," I growled, grabbing a quick peek over the counter.

She stood beside display racks long emptied of donuts, muffins, and their sweet selections of seasonal cookies. Her dark hair had been tied back, hidden behind a thick furred hood.

"Put it on the counter, then step away." She sighted down the barrel of a semi-automatic rifle, a scowl on her thin lips. The gun twitched. "You have ten seconds."

I cradled the cup closer, enjoying its warmth. I couldn't remember a single day since the comet hit and the Siidi invaded that I'd felt this happy. I wasn't going to give this up.

"Sneaky trick, dropping a giant ice ball on the planet. Think they're out there, in town? I haven't seen one of the squid-faced bastards in weeks."

Steam rose into the icy air like smoke from a genie bottle, conjuring fond memories of a life before suffering. I missed the hustle and bustle of humanity. I missed the daily grind, the crowds, and even the lines where I'd read the paper and waited for some pimple-faced kid to pour me a cup of cocoa to take the chill off a late December morning.

"I thought the city was empty." Her tone sounded cautious. "You from around here?"

I laughed, hard and long, the tension exploding out of me. It'd been months since I'd spoken to anyone. "That was the worst pickup line I'd heard since doomsday."

She fired a round into the counter above my head. "Better?"

"Sorry!" I ducked, the humor gone. "My social skills are a little rusty."

"The cocoa, give it up." She wasn't any smoother.

"I was visiting when it happened. My name's John."

"Cassandra," she said. "And I want that drink."

"I didn't expect to see anyone. The ground fighting's been rough, but it's moved out of the northeast. The Siidi are smart, but not as sneaky as we are."

"I've been here too long to leave, invasion or not." The barrel of her gun dipped a few inches. "You got people?"

"No. . . not anymore." I tried not to think of what I'd lost.

"Me neither."

It suddenly felt colder in the little shop than the impact of winter falling outside. I didn't want to think about the past or the things I'd seen or done since the Siidi landed. I'd lost everyone. The world was a different place now, frigid, lonely, and dangerous.

A faint sizzling squeal rippled through the air outside, the noise of Siidi weapons charging. That sound would echo through my nightmares. They *were* out there, somewhere.

Cassandra vanished behind the display rack. My heart stuttered. I held my breath, instinctively shielding the hot chocolate. We weren't as alone in town as I'd thought.

The sound faded into the icy air.

"Nice chatting." Cassandra crept around the corner, jittery again. "But I think I'll take my cocoa to go now."

The hot paper cup made my skin tingle. This beverage represented a world I'd never see again, a warmer time of sitting beside the fire, chatting with good friends, and enjoying life. How long would it be before I held something like this again?

"I can't let it go, Cassandra. I *need* this."

"*I* need it more." Her voice boomed through the abandoned shop like the growling of an angry bear.

"Share it with me?" I asked. "Let's sit like two civilized people and have some cocoa together."

"Now who's spouting bad pickup lines?" She frowned, but she lowered the gun. "Find a cup and put the chocolate on that table over there. I'll do the pouring. Don't expect any marshmallow."

"Bossy, I like that." I wasn't sure I'd have been able to let it go if she'd said no.

"Don't get cute. It's cocoa, not a date."

I raised the cup as if it were a sacred relic. A chipped demitasse lay against an overturned display. It looked like a thimble as I picked it up and placed it beside the steaming cup. It wouldn't be much, but I'd take what I could get.

Cassandra eased into the chair opposite, rifle held awkwardly across her chest. Her fingers shook, and I was amazed at how thin she appeared. Food had gotten scarce, but I'd managed to scavenge enough. It hadn't occurred to me that others might not be so fortunate.

"Maybe we should have dinner together after all."

"Drink." She cradled the cup as if holding an infant, her dark eyes distant and moist. I almost cried when I noticed she'd given me some of the marshmallow after all.

I glanced through the shop. It had the same blasted and abandoned look as almost everything these days. The racks had been looted, and machinery destroyed. Everything that had made this place special had either been shattered or rusted away. Now that I had time to observe, something felt out of place. I stared at the cocoa and then at Cassandra. A chill ran down my spine.

"No power. Everything's broken," I said slowly, my heart racing, my breath puffing in quick billowing clouds.

"Yeah. . ." Her lips had barely kissed the rim of the cup. "So?"

“How’d you make this?”

Her eyes widened. “I thought you did.”

I drank quickly as a faint sizzling squeal rippled through the air.

For Those Who Suffer from Consciousness

by Kurt Newton

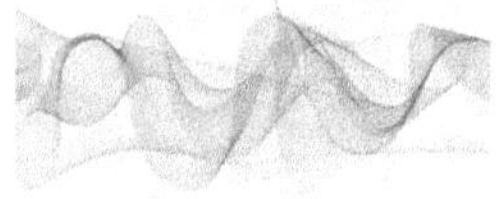

Hirais had a way with knives. Okkum was a sufferer, best known by his blood, which painted the edge of the sidewalk and spilled into the gutter. His particular form of performance art had left its mark around the city.

For those who walked the streets every day, Hirais and Okkum had become somewhat of a nuisance, their act as engaging as two dogs locked in copulation. But for the tourist—the traveler naive to local custom—it was always a shocking sight: Okkum chained to a linden tree, Hirais skinning him alive.

Hirais and Okkum had learned to expect one of two reactions from first timers. Most would stand in stunned silence, alarmed that nothing was being done to stop the gruesome display. These were the spectators. In the second category were the heroes. Occasionally, a brave soul would take it upon themself and rush to stop Hirais, knocking him to the ground and taking the blade from his hand. Hirais would not resist. When Okkum would laugh at the spectacle, the hero would not find it funny.

"Why did you stop him?" Okkum would invariably ask.

The hero would become confused. "To save you. You're bleeding," the hero would say. Okkum would then look the hero straight in the eye. "We are all bleeding. It was right of you to stop him. But once you leave, he will continue to do what he does. And you will become like them." Okkum would then nod to the passersby, mostly locals, who would cast looks of disdain.

The hero would understand then that they had become a pawn in some sadistic passion play. Then one of two things would happen. Either the hero would become angered and say things like "You people are all the same" or "I hope you kill each other" and walk away, proving Okkum's hypothesis. Or, the hero would get up, apologize for interrupting, and, in order to appease their embarrassment, would drop a few coins in the cup that sat nearby. Also, proving Okkum's hypothesis.

Hirais and Okkum were always gracious, folding hands and nodding appreciatively, as the street scene returned to normal.

This went on for many months and even years. Until one day.

The sky was an overcast grey. Hirais and Okkum had chosen an abandoned street cart to perform their improvised death scene. Okkum was chained to the cart's wheel. Hirais had already cut a pattern across Okkum's back and had peeled the skin from his left calf muscle. Okkum's blood spread onto the street like a spill of crimson dye. A woman approached them with a pale complexion. She had the shadow of ghosts beneath her eyes. Quite unexpectedly, she sat down beside Okkum and hugged him, unmindful of the blood staining her clothes. She hugged him as a mother would hug a child.

Okkum, who was always quick with a remark, let the moment pass in silence. He hugged the woman back. Hirais took the opportunity to sharpen his blade. At last, Okkum and the woman broke their embrace. The woman was the first to speak.

"I get it," she said. "When the dog suffers from consciousness, the better its meat will be." She rolled up her sleeves and nodded to Hirais. "Go ahead."

Hirais and Okkum exchanged looks. Okkum nodded. Hirais held the woman's outstretched arm and cut a diagonal across her skin. Blood welled and ran in tiny rivers until droplets of her blood joined Okkum's. Hirais did the same to the woman's other arm and she sat on the edge of the sidewalk, arms lowered to the street gutter, bleeding.

The grey clouds overhead thinned and a ray of sunshine briefly poked through.

Okkum smiled, feeling the warmth on his face, and hope in his heart for the first time in a very long while.

The Exchange Student

by Kurt Newton

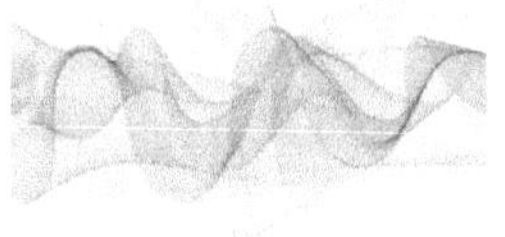

The exchange student arrives at your doorstep weighed down with clothes bags and small kitchen appliances. Dark liquid eyes stare up at you out of a small tan face.

"I'm the exchange student, is this—"

You interrupt. "Yes, hi. Please put your things over there. I'm Mark."

"My name is Hachnahmed Amenhachbed," the student coughs, the cough sounding more like a name than his real one. "My friends call me 'Ahmed.'"

You don't know why this boy has chosen your doorstep. It could be that you drink a little too much and forgot that you signed up for foreign exchange student housing at the local high school. It could be the board of education felt sorry for you because you lost your wife and child in a horrible school bus accident. It could be that Ahmed just has the wrong address. But you let him in anyway.

Ahmed turns out to be a big help around the house, washing dishes, vacuuming, and preparing odd, exotic meals from the rather bland food fare that occupies your cabinets. You have no complaints at all, except for Ahmed's personal hygiene, which leaves something to be desired.

In the days that follow, you expect Ahmed to unpack his belongings and go to class, but he doesn't even leave the house. He doesn't change his clothes, let alone brush his teeth. When he's not completing the household chores, he simply sits in one of the unused chairs and stares as you go about your daily routine. Sometimes he takes notes.

You yourself don't work—you haven't since the accident. But you do run errands now and then. There are times you have gone out to restock your supply of peanut butter and coffee—every meal Ahmed creates has some degree of peanut butter or coffee in it—and have come home to find Ahmed still sitting in the same position as before you left. Sometimes his eyes are closed as if meditating. There is an odd whistle that emanates from his nostrils. One day you think to move in closer for a better listen, but his eyes suddenly pop open, sending your heart up into your throat.

"My name is Hachnahmed Amenhachbed!" he shouts. "My friends call me 'Ahmed.'" Then he smiles, white teeth gleaming.

He must be brushing when I'm not looking, you think, and ask him what's for dinner.

As the days pass, you forget to ask your questions of why Ahmed doesn't go to class, or when he will be going back to where he came from. He seems quite content to be your personal house servant and cook. And his company is better than the talking heads on the television set. But then maybe you don't ask because you're afraid of what he might tell you. Maybe Ahmed's idea of 'exchange student' is entirely different than the accepted European definition. Maybe Ahmed has been sent to look after you. But then maybe you drink a little too much to think, act, or believe rationally in anything anymore. And therefore, anything is possible.

A month passes. You find that you no longer shave or shower. You have become very thin on the diet of food Ahmed has been cooking. But you don't feel weak. In fact, your body has hardened to a healthy musculature. Your teeth remain remarkably white. Your errands no longer have meaning. There is only one thing on your mind.

It's late. You go to Ahmed's bedroom and find him sitting on top of the covers. His nose is whistling. His eyes flash open as you approach, and for the first time you see something more behind that gaze than was there previously.

"My name is Hachnahmed Amenhachbed," he says. "My friends call me 'Ahmed.'" He smiles. "Are you ready, now, Mr. Mark?" he asks.

"Yes, I believe I am," you tell him, and Ahmed nods.

You take a drive into the night. Ahmed is at the wheel. He seems to know exactly where you want to go. The cemetery looms into view. Ahmed stays in the car. "Goodbye my friend," you hear him utter as you get out of the car and take a walk.

You arrive at the footstep of your wife and child's grave. You shrug off the life that has weighed you down like so many clothes bags and small kitchen appliances. The darkness of the ground's eyes stares up at you. You burrow headfirst into the dirt, unable to breathe (not wanting to). Your body is firm and rigid. You disappear to a comfortable depth. You touch wood (you recall they were buried together). You furrow up alongside, testing your memory, testing your strength.

You knock, and they let you in.

It Could've Been Worse

by Gabriella Balcom

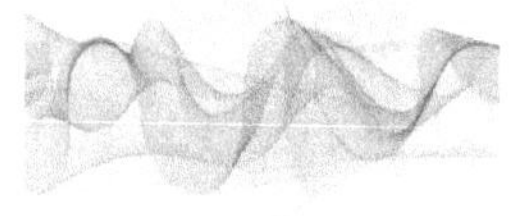

After parking his tractor in the barn, Fred turned it off and wiped the sweat from his forehead with his handkerchief. The heat wasn't the only thing bothering him, though. His workday had been much longer than usual. It had been harder than most, too, what with the strange holes he'd discovered on the acreage he'd plowed and readied for planting yesterday. Priding himself on his down-to-earth, no-nonsense approach to life, he knew he hadn't overlooked them, and holes couldn't just appear out of nowhere, but there they'd been. Strangely, they reminded him of pictures he'd seen of moon craters.

Over the past few months, other farmers in town had discovered the same thing, some of them suggesting asteroids had fallen. Fred had snorted at that idea. He had a different, more logical theory, suspecting pesky neighborhood kids were to blame, finding a new way to pull pranks.

They'd certainly cost him valuable time today, forcing him to till the ground again. He'd worried about loose pockets of earth deep down, or something else he couldn't see, so he'd gone over the same area several times before leveling it back out.

Fred stepped down from his tractor and felt something move under his feet. Losing his balance, he fell, landing on a rake. He yelled out at the sudden pain in his stomach as the tines punctured his skin. Stumbling to his feet, he felt light-headed and swayed. When he raised his shirt and gingerly touched the small wounds, his fingertips came away red.

"Dang," he muttered. "Well, it could've been worse."

Fog rolled into the barn—a typical occurrence, given the nearby lake—and wafted past him. It reached the rake and hovered, drifting back and forth above the bloody tines.

The movement reminded the watching man of a cat rubbing against a scratching post or luxuriating in a patch of catnip or a sunny spot on the ground. But he snorted at his own whimsy and turned his attention back to his belly.

Fred, dabbing at his wounds with his handkerchief, didn't notice the fog changing color from a translucent grey to a faint reddish tinge.

He trod heavily toward the open doorway, but gasped, stopping abruptly. His eyes widened, and he reached to touch his back where a scythe was embedded between his shoulder blades, his sweaty, light-green shirt darkening.

The nearby wall covered with tools and farm equipment shimmered faintly, and a machete flew from its hook, striking Fred's right shoulder with an audible thunk. A hoe rose from where it leaned against a pile of pallets, flipping blade-side up. It soared toward the man, the blade impaling his forehead, and blood ran down his face.

More tools left the wall, striking and slashing Fred's body. A pair of shears pierced his neck, going straight through to the other side.

His mouth gaped open in a scream, but all he could manage was a faint gurgle. He collapsed on the ground, blood pooling around him.

Tools dropped beside him, landing in the blood, and the red pool grew smaller and smaller until no trace of it remained.

A thump signaled a door shutting somewhere close by.

"Where are you, Fred?" a man called from outside the barn. "You big lug, you haven't forgotten our plans, have you?"

"You ready for a nice, cold beer?" another man asked. "We are."

All the tools rose from the ground. Soaring through the air, they repositioned themselves

where they'd been previously just as Fred's
buddies walked into the barn.

Box 27

by Kevin Lauderdale

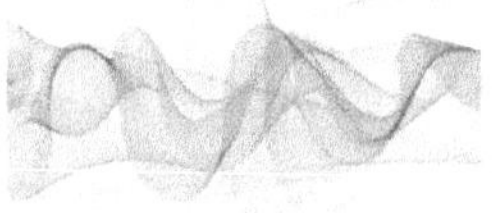

"Welcome to Galactic Confederation processing. Please state your name."

The creature behind the counter — they used actual counters, even this deep in the heart of the Galaxy — looked like a giant chartreuse bear with black fins running down her spine. Marta assumed the bear was a she. The translator certainly produced a female voice. The bear wasn't wearing a name tag or anything.

"Ambassador Marta Rilla-Chen," Marta replied clearly and directly. "Of the Earth Diplomatic Corps." She was there to present her credentials to the Confederation. But the ceremony wasn't being held in a throne room or a hall bedecked with ceremonial splendor. She was in an office of some sort, whose multiple counters and flickering lighting reminded her of the fluorescents in the D.M.V. back home. Only the view of the swirling Galactic core out of the windows and the presence of dozens of different types of aliens around her broke the illusion. Still, she couldn't help but wonder if some of those other aliens in the office were there to pay parking tickets.

"Form, please," growled the bear in a bored monotone, and Marta handed over the flexiplast pages. The bear ran her eyes down the form. She stamped an item here and circled an item there with a laser pen. She stopped and looked up from the form. With pronounced disapproval, she said, "You didn't fill in Box 27."

Marta had been expecting that. "Right," she said, "I wasn't sure what to put down. What does 'Society Code' mean?"

The bear sighed. "Every member species has a specific number and name." Marta found the droning quality of her rough voice actually quite charming. The bear had given this speech, what, a thousand times before? That's how many member worlds were in the Confederation. "We'll assign your catalog number, but you need to provide the name you will all be known by."

Marta felt confused. Her face must have shown it.

The bear said, "I can see we'll have to go through the whole *zarfasnop*. Let's try to make this quick. Says here your planet's name is Earth. Does that mean anything in particular?"

"Umm, land, soil, dirt."

"Oh yeah. I've heard about your planet. Earth is the place with all the water, but you named it Dirt. Makes a lot of sense. How about if you call yourselves 'The Crazies.' That's short at least. Raljevanites call themselves, 'We Who Created the Ice-Based Food That Is Sweet But Causes Your Head To Hurt.' That's their planet's claim to fame, and they're sticking with it for all it's worth. If you were from Melton II, you would be part of, 'The Survivors.' That's nice. Also, short. Anyway, 'The Crazies,' then?" Her pen hovered over the form.

"Wait!" cried Marta. *The Crazies!* She could just hear her boss exploding over that. Forget her boss — the 8 billion people of Earth would not be pleased that the rest of the Galaxy would know them as *The Crazies.* "Let's try something else. Umm, we also call ourselves Terrans."

"What does that mean?"

"People who live on Terra . . . Oh, but that just means land."

"Which is dirt. 'The Dirties?'"

Marta shook her head. "Oh! Of course! We call ourselves *People.*" Why hadn't she thought of that in the first place? That was better. That was respectable.

The bear snorted. "Everyone calls themselves People. My people call themselves, People. That guy over there from Aquatox IV wearing the glass bowl that keeps his head immersed in water, calls his fellow creatures, People. You'll have to try harder."

Marta thought. "All right. We are. . . *Homo sapiens*. The Wise Man. And Woman. Technically we're *Homo sapiens sapiens*. So how about The Really Wise People?"

"Didn't your planet almost blow itself up with nuclear weapons —"

"But we didn't."

"— and then almost destroy itself through overheating?"

"But we didn't." Still, she could see the bear's point. Humans had eventually mastered atomic power constructively, restored the planet's ecology, and made it to the stars. Now they were even joining a confederation of fellow spacefarers. We had come far, but perhaps it was stretching it a bit to wish to be known as *Really Wise.*

"Besides," said the bear. "The 'Really Wise People' is already taken."

"By whom?" Marta was indignant. Who could be so egotistical as to actually use that?

The bear gave a wry, growling chuckle. "*My* People."

Marta shook her long black hair and composed herself. "All right. . . oh! The Humans!"

"What does that mean?"

Marta sighed. "People."

"Your species has a real talent for circular thought. You want to reconsider *The Crazies*?"

"No." Marta closed her eyes and concentrated hard. Humans were indeed crazy, dirty, noisy, lovable, brilliant, joyous . . . Marta wasn't getting anywhere. This was frustrating. She looked at the bear. "What's your name?" She couldn't keep on thinking of this 'Really Wise' Person as a bear.

"Why do you want to know?"

"It's what humans do. We connect."

"I am called Weylo."

"Hi, Weylo." Marta smiled. "Truth is, we humans don't really know who we are. We're just beginning to figure that out. That's partly why we're out here. Each of us is a human, but we're really at our best when we're connected. It's the things we do together that make us Humanity."

"Humanity?"

"Yeah, Humanity." That was it. It meant not just all of us, but all of us connected.

"At least it's short." Was that a smile on Weylo's muzzle? She gave the form one final, resounding stamp. "Welcome to the Galactic Confederation, Marta Rilla-Chen. . . and Humanity."

Forget Me Not Inc.

by Anthony Self

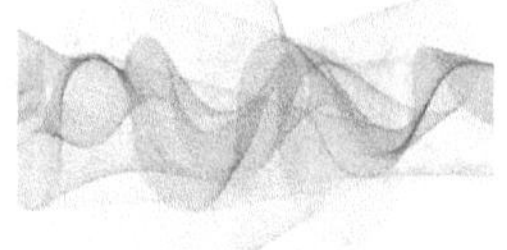

The girl wanted to forget the last month of her life.

Spencer sat across from the sobbing girl in her living room. He focused on a piece of dirt on the coffee table between them. He wondered about licking his thumb and scrubbing it. Decided against it. It was the last day of his assessment, after all.

Cobb's mouth quirked in a half-bitter, half-humorous line. "Perhaps you'd like to reconsider?"

His handler for today was a little man, not quite fat, with round glasses that seemed too small for his large, domed head that appeared to shine like a varnished football. Every word was enunciated with a gravitas that Spencer likened to that of a Headmaster. A fire and brimstone stickler for details.

Cobb never stuttered nor hesitated with his words. Spencer knew that on his last day, he would need to adhere strictly to the protocols of the company. They hadn't assigned Cobb to him without reason. As Spencer listened to Cobb speak to the girl about the itinerary of what the service would provide, he couldn't help but feel like an imposter during this procedure. Like a vulture waiting for the kill.

Cobb had asked a question he hadn't caught. He cursed himself for his mind wandering; Cobb was the type of guy who would file a lapse like that in a mental mind palace for later consideration.

"Sorry?"

Cobb glanced at the pamphlet on the table with the instructions from the company. Spencer swiped it away and put it in his suit pocket. They couldn't leave any evidence behind.

The girl collected herself and stared mournfully at the opened case on the coffee table. If Willy Wonka had made a briefcase, this would be it. It was the sort of purple that children's dreams were made of. Spencer couldn't help but imagine that there was forbidden chocolate within.

In a way, there was.

Cobb deftly arced his arm around the opened case and pointed with a chubby digit at the protective high-density foam of the interior. "The green pill is for a day, the yellow for a week, the orange for a month, and so on," he said in a practised voice. "After consuming the pill, you'll receive a call in half an hour from one of our doctors. They will explain that you were involved in a minor collision and experienced a concussion. At first, you may have some discombobulation, but that will soon pass."

The girl nodded. She'd read the instructions. By the look of her, Spencer assumed she'd stayed up all night analyzing every word. He mildly wondered what color briefcase he would receive after the assessment. Every handler had a different color.

She plucked the orange pill from the foamed interior and held it aloft.

"It may have only been a month, but the bastard broke my heart," she said before swallowing it whole.

Cobb nodded sagely. He quickly shut the lid and did a final scan of the room.

"In a few minutes, you'll start to feel lightheaded," he said. Smiling at her with a distracted, going-in-several-directions-at-once smile. "You'll feel like you're in a state of Nirvana and then come to right here on your sofa. We'll leave now, as you'll likely be startled by two strangers sitting in your living room. Good day."

Cobb patted Spencer's leg to indicate they were leaving. Spencer wondered how long the old man had been doing this. Cobb checked his watch.

"Let's get something to eat," he said flatly.

An introspective mood had fallen over the two suited men as they sat drinking in the pub. It was a fancy place, a sort of minimalist-classical that Spencer would normally avoid. He imagined that in the evenings hundreds of conversations would be told in there with loud voices, all of them competing and vying for attention.

When they had first entered, Spencer was adamant that he would order a soda water with lime to show the older handler that he didn't drink during working hours, but when Cobb nonchalantly ordered a pint, he assumed it was fair game and duly requested a whiskey and coke.

"Bit early for the strong stuff, isn't it?" Cobb asked in a soft, contemptuous voice.

Spencer felt his cheeks flush.

Cobb shrugged in a dismissive way, and they found themselves a booth in the near-empty pub. The reflective moment came after they regarded the menus.

"What did you think of the last client?" Cobb asked casually. There was something innately foreign about his tone that rang a warning bell with Spencer. He'd spent the last couple of hours with the man, but this felt forced. Spencer prided himself on being able to size someone just by spending a few minutes with them, and Cobb didn't seem to be the kind of person to ask other's opinions.

Spencer looked up from his menu. *They'll always test you,* a voice whispered in his head. *Never let your guard down. Even when you think you're on the home stretch. Remember that.*

Spencer had done his homework. For clients who had made reservations for their treatment, a file about them had been collated by the company. From their spouses, siblings, parents, and friends, every intimate detail about their life had been chronicled for the handlers prior to their meeting. It was the only way they could do what they did without any repercussions. Spencer knew, for example, that when the sobbing girl was thirteen, she ran a razor blade down her arm because Billy DeMarco from school didn't ask her to prom.

"I think she'll be using our services again," he said tactfully.

"There are some," Cobb said after a moment of closely scrutinizing Spencer, "that regard what we do as blasphemous. Abhorrent. That people need both the good and the bad to learn and grow. Do you agree?"

Spencer shifted uncomfortably in the booth. He cleared his throat.

"That's not my decision to make," he finally said. "It raises the question of whether human experience is little more than the aggregate of a person's memories, or if experience constructs and defines a person whether they remember it or not. Would erasing a terrible experience make us happier, or would it change who we are? Not for me to decide. That's the client's choice."

Cobb stared at Spencer icily. He grunted then, raised his eyebrows, and waved the waiter over. He ordered a B.L.T. and Spencer ordered pasta. They ate in silence, and then, it was time for their next client of the day.

"Listen, it wasn't my fault the stupid bitch ran out into the road, was it?"

Spencer regarded the lawyer with mild detestation. He eyed the walls and hangings with a cool, professional eye. The lawyer considered himself a connoisseur of canvas artistry, leather-bound tomes, and sculptures of monstrous proportions, but Spencer heard the querulous tone in his voice. The man was scared.

Cobb sat on one of the expensive designer seats, a tumbler of the finest scotch and his purple briefcase before him. The lawyer was pacing, talking to himself more than anyone else.

"I mean, do you know what would happen to me if anyone found out? I'd be disbarred." He stopped, turned to the suited men, and clenched his hand into a fist in dramatic fashion. "Disbarred. I put criminals away, did you know that? Scum from the streets, killing and raping, and all kinds of heinous acts." He cupped his face into his hands. Spencer found the routine tiresome. "What good would it do anyone if I couldn't do my job anymore?"

The guy thinks we're in court, Spencer mused. *He's trying to appease us.*

"We're not here to judge," Cobb said, as if reading Spencer's mind. His deep, slow voice seemed to command the room, whereas the lawyer looked like his ass was on sideways, and he needed to shit really bad. "I take it you have taken the necessary precautions to . . . ."

The lawyer waved a dismissive hand. "Yeah, yeah. Got rid of the motor and the . . . uh . . . body. Listen, this only happened yesterday, okay? I don't need to give you any details of people I've seen before that, right? I need to make sure the least amount of people getting a card saying I've participated in this . . . service is kept to a minimum."

Cobb smiled. To the lawyer, it would have looked like a smile that said: *I am the one person on this earth you can bring your problems to.* But for Spencer, he felt an ominous presence behind that smile. That smile had teeth. Shark's teeth.

"I can assure you that the company has taken care of every eventuality. It's good that you came to us as soon as you did." Cobb stood up and took the green pill from the case. He handed it to the lawyer and nodded.

"Will it matter if I have a line before I take this?" The lawyer asked.

Cobb flashed that predatory smile again. "Sure thing. In ten minutes, you won't even remember you've taken it."

In the car, Cobb turned to Spencer.

"Tough few weeks, eh?"

The alarm bell rang in Spencer's ears again. "I can only hope I've proved myself worthy for the company."

Cobb nodded as if he understood. "It's not for everyone, you know."

Spencer took a moment to absorb this. "Can I ask you something? Off the record?"

Cobb steered the car through the streets, staring ahead. "I never knew we were on the record, Spencer."

Shit, shit, shit.

Spencer silently cursed himself for the slip. It was something he'd said a million times over the years. *They'll always test you,* his editor had said. *Never let your guard down. Even when you think you're on the home stretch. Remember that.*

"I mean, I assume the company pulled out the big guns for my final day of assessment. That was the last client of the day, right? So . . . I take it you've made up your mind. Either I made the cut, or I didn't. Just thought asking a question after the fact might be okay."

Cobb continued driving. He left a long delay before answering, pushing his glasses up his nose.

"Ask your question."

Spencer looked out the window. The evening sun was starting to set — the sky was a cherry bruise. "Do you think what we do is good?"

Cobb regarded this for a moment before answering briskly: "Yes. Yes I do."

They continued to drive silently for a few moments before he elaborated. "Used to be a time when everyone in the world got offended by the slightest thing. A comment on YouTube. Gender-swapping in a film. The accepted pronoun on people's Twitter feeds. Trivial things, really. But it conveyed a deeper sense of what people really were experiencing. Grief. Fear. The unknown. We bring harmony to an unequal battleground, Spencer. If ignorance is bliss, then sign me up for that religion. Because it's better than the inevitable. That's what I think."

Spencer continued looking out the window.

"But on that note," Cobb said, "you're wrong. We've got one more client to see."

Spencer unconsciously flinched. He'd read up on all the files for that day. The lawyer had been the last. He was sure of it. This was another test. Or maybe he'd been rumbled.

"Oh?" he said, trying to sound calm.

"I said this job isn't for everyone," Cobb said, with a world-weary tone of emptiness. "Maybe you'll appreciate the harmony I'm talking about after."

They drove for the remainder of the journey in silence.

"You're the first!" The woman said excitedly as she opened the door. She wore a filthy sweater with a reindeer leaping across a crib with a green background. Several homemade necklaces hung pendulously from her neck to her plump breasts, all ending with crude twig-shaped T crosses.

Spencer arched his eyebrows. An odor of something like spoiled meat wafted past them. If Cobb smelled it, he didn't react. A few flies zigzagged ponderously from the main door to the outside world.

Cobb smiled politely, his purple briefcase weighing like an anchor by his knees.

The woman looked at Spencer and then at Cobb. For a moment there was a vacant look in her eyes, but then, she blinked with the surprised, pleased look of someone who had just recalled something that had been out of her mind far too long.

"You're here to see the baby Jesus?"

Spencer looked at Cobb.

"Indeed, we are," Cobb replied courteously.

The woman beamed a wide PR smile and extended the front door open. Cobb nodded and went into the hallway. Spencer followed. The pungent cloying stench of rotten vegetables and decomposition heightened the further they walked down the narrow hallway. Various pictures of the Lord and Savior adorned the darkened walls. Spencer heard the distinct buzz of flies as they ricocheted from wall to wall.

"A tad hot in here, no?" Spencer remarked.

"Oh, that's how he likes it!" The woman chortled. They continued down the long, narrow hallway. "My little Jesus just loves the heat. Have the radiators on twenty-four-seven. It's how he shows his *miracles*."

Cobb turned and furrowed his brow as Spencer lifted his hand to cup his nose and mouth.

"*They* said it wouldn't happen. But I knew. I knew!" the woman howled. They followed her through the darkened tunnel until they entered the living room.

When Spencer saw the monstrosity on the wall he turned and retched.

The baby couldn't have been more than six months old. Naked as the day it was born, the bulbous purple legs were the first thing his eyes were drawn to. Gravity had completed its innocuous work, and the blood had drained to the bottom-most part of the body. Flies in the room circled languidly in a fluid motion. A small, blue tongue hung like a slug from its mouth. Several candles were still lit before the crucifixion shrine.

A paralysis came over Spencer. His legs became elastic, and he focused on the worn carpet, a beige color of undescriptive quality and texture.

Just focus on one spot, he told himself. *What you saw wasn't real. Couldn't be real. No sane person could do that to a child.*

He felt a hand clamp on his shoulder.

"Wait outside," Cobb said coldly. "I'll be out shortly."

The woman clapped her hands together.

"Did you bring Myrrh?"

Spencer wiped the remnants of sickness from his mouth.

Cobb came over, with two bottles of water. He sat by Spencer and took a long swig.

"Jesus, Cobb . . . its eyes. The eyes had disintegrated. How long had it been . . . hung there?"

Cobb shrugged. "Maybe a week. Maybe more. The company will deal with it. I gave her a sedative. They'll remove everything, and then, she'll take her pill."

Spencer unscrewed the cap and greedily drank.

Cobb surveyed with abject dismay. "I told you it wasn't for everyone."

Spencer laughed. It was the sound of a madman. "That was insane. *No one* should ever have to see that."

Cobb looked at Spencer, for the first time. Looked at him through his round glasses, through his squat, wide frame. Looked at him as a person.

"And yet this is the job we do. Bringing harmony to an unequal battleground."

Cobb looked down at Spencer's shirt. The two opened buttons. Slowly and deferentially, he opened the other two below. Exposing the wire. Spencer didn't resist.

"The company knew, Spencer," Cobb said, matter-of-factly. "They always knew. In a way, I think they wanted you to do your exposé. But in the end, the house always wins."

Spencer nodded. He suddenly felt quite sanguine and happy.

Cobb came close, whispering into his ear as he detached the wire from his chest. "Handlers are already going through your home, taking any material from the last two weeks. I know you made hard drives, but we'll find them. That's what we do. The company wanted me to give you a lesson . . . regress you back to a child-like state. But I see potential in you, Spencer. You're going to lose five years. Before the journalism . . . before they molded you. That's my gift to you. I don't think that's a bad thing, overall. I think you'll still have that curios intent."

Spencer blinked. He made the sloppy hand motions of an incbriated drunk when the last orders were called, but he didn't fight too much. He felt that this was the way things were supposed to go. He smiled at Cobb.

"The pill was in the water I just gave you, Spencer. Once again, I apologize. In a few minutes, you'll start to feel lightheaded." He said, smiling at him in a distracted, going-in-several-directions-at-once smile. "You'll feel like you're in a state of Nirvana and then come to, right here outside this house. I'll leave now, as you'll likely be startled by a stranger sitting beside you. Good day."

Spencer couldn't remember the man's name. He felt a euphoric state that the world should be unified within any conflict, saw his interpretation of God, and then passed out.

When he jolted awake, he found himself on a street. He didn't remember how he got there.

The Valley of the Masks

by Pedro Iniguez

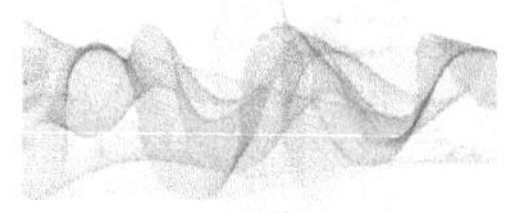

In the dim light of the cave, Kiyana's mother pursed her lips as her hand probed her wrinkled, purple skin. The sight and feel of Kiyana's flesh—marked by liver spots and fine, prickly hairs—caused the old woman to wince. Her mother then regarded her own misshapen purple skin and continued the inspection.

"Spread your arms," her mother said.

Kiyana raised her arms outward. Her skin sagged heaviest below her underarms creating long dangling pouches. Her mother gauged her height, made mental notes as to where to trim, and proceeded to alter old bits of fabric to accommodate her small frame.

When she was done, her mother draped long blue robes over her daughter until not one inch of purple skin was visible. Then came the gloves to cover her gnarled, bony fingers.

"Is it comfortable?" her mother asked.

Kiyana nodded.

Her mother swept aside a tuft of Kiyana's hair and placed an ivory mask gently over her head.

"Why do I have to wear this?" Kiyana said.

"We've been through this," her mother said, adjusting the mask so that Kiyana's eyes lined up through the holes. "The guards at the valley won't permit purple-skins to enter the river nor the hunting grounds. Only Blues and Reds are allowed to hunt or retrieve water. We wear their ceremonial masks and garbs to hide ourselves so that we may bring back sustenance."

"Why?"

Her mother shook her head. "Because the Great God Malovex decreed it ages ago. Purple skin is unsightly and frowned upon."

"But we can't help the way we're born," Kiyana said.

Her mother said nothing.

Kiyana brought her fingers to the mask, running them along the faceted jewels lining the forehead like a crown. "How did you acquire this mask?"

"Never ask me that." Her mother stepped back to look at Kiyana. She nodded. "Now that your father has transitioned into the void, it is your duty to bring back what we need." The mother hobbled toward an empty pail and handed it to Kiyana. "We need water. Go to the river and fetch us some. The valley lies just below the mountain. Travel safely."

Kiyana nodded and embraced her mother.

Outside, dozens of caves lined the side of the mountain where other Purples ambled about in the humid afternoon. A few dug into the earth with their hands, shoveling what insects they could find into their mouths. Some licked the scattered droplets of dew still clinging to the rock face. Many appeared gaunt, and starved, their ribs jutting from their sides.

Above, the clouds began rolling inward, blotting out both suns.

Kiyana treaded slowly down the mountain, planting her feet evenly where the soil wasn't loose. On a few occasions, she slipped and tumbled along the rocks. She ignored the pain and carried onward.

At the foot of the mountain, the valley opened before her revealing a lush plain sprawling with ferns and milkweeds and palms. Ripe yellow fruits budded from the trees along her path, where they hung low enough to pluck.

Further ahead where the tree line opened up, she heard the roar of the river. She managed to smile as she pictured the running streams of water. In all ten revolutions of her life, she'd yet to see the river. She'd only seen the reflective sparkle of water inside a moldy bucket or when it rained and spilled on the earth as it bled into the clay.

Two large men draped in red robes watched her approach the banks of the river where a line of Reds and Blues had formed. The guards wore ivory masks similar to hers and brandished long spears like her father used to carry on his hunts. They nodded and allowed her to walk past, returning their gazes toward the front of the queue.

Kiyana shuffled toward the back of the line, where Blues and Reds intermingled, gossiping on matters she didn't understand. They all wore ivory masks of varying designs. Some were decorated with jewels, while others displayed gold accents etched into their frames. Many people wore plain masks, which had begun to reveal slight cracks along the eyes. They all, however, wore robes that corresponded to the color of their skin.

She thought about her own skin crossed her arms and bowed her head, hoping no one would expose her for what she truly was. The feeling of shame and guilt began to fester in the pit of her belly, burning her insides like the days she'd gone without food.

On a small island in the middle of the river, a sole marble statue dwarfed everybody in its presence. The sculpture represented the likeness of a tall and muscular man brandishing a spear, its tip aimed at the sky. The man's skin was taught and free of welts and scarring. His face was covered by an ornate mask far more bejeweled than any Kiyana had seen. His presence made her insides twist into knots.

A pair of hands clutched her shoulders from behind. "Isn't Malovex wonderful, child?"

Kiyana turned. A Blue woman looked upon the statue in admiration.

"Indeed," Kiyana said. "He is very big."

The woman laughed. "Among other things, yes. He is also wise and all-knowing." A gust of cold wind swept through the riverbank, and Kiyana could feel the cold penetrate her gown and sting her skin like small razors. In the sky, the dark clouds drew nearer. "We here are fortunate to be among his chosen, to bask in the glory of his river and the bounty of his game."

"Of course," Kiyana said. "We are very fortunate that there is so much for us to take. There appears to be plenty to share with everyone."

"Oh no," the woman said, wagging her finger. "This bounty is not meant for the Purples that plague the mountainside. They are ugly, wicked, lawless people. This valley is our refuge from those monsters."

Kiyana felt her face flush. She was glad the mask was there to cover her shame. "When did Malovex decree these laws?" Kiyana asked not knowing what more to say.

"Oh, it's been ages," the woman said. "No one alive really knows but it is the law of the land, and laws are meant to be followed."

A ruckus erupted behind them. The guards sprang into a bush, jabbing their spears into the thicket with wild abandon. A small figure leapt from the shrubs and darted past the men and into the ranks of those waiting in line.

The intruder was a little girl, younger than Kiyana herself, bare-faced and wearing tattered clothes revealing patches of purple skin underneath.

"Please help me," the little girl pleaded. Her face drooped in certain places, and patches of hair lined her scalp like dying grass.

The crowd gasped, many stepping away from the girl.

"I only need some water for my family."

The guards spun and sprinted toward the child.

The girl scanned the masked faces, her palms open and facing outward, begging. A few Blues and Reds turned away. Others stared back in what Kiyana assumed to be curiosity.

The guards planted their feet and cocked their spears. Kiyana jumped in between the girl and her pursuers, wrapping an arm around the child.

The guards retracted their spears.

"Move," one of the guards barked. "This one has trespassed on sacred ground and must be executed."

"But," Kiyana said, "She only wants some water. She can have some of mine."

The crowd murmured in disgust, the line now fragmented as the people sought to gain distance from Kiyana and the child.

"What's this?" said the guard. "A Purple sympathizer?"

"There's plenty enough here to share with her," Kiyana said.

The guard slowly lifted Kiyana's mask with the tip of his spear. The crowd howled and hissed.

"Another Purple," Someone yelled.

"Sacrilege!" belted another.

Kiyana's heart raced, thumping and burning like a hot coal inside her chest.

The guards approached, their spears shaking in their grasp.

Kiyana stepped back, pulling the little girl alongside her. Suddenly, drops of rain began to pelt Kiyana as a storm fell upon the valley.

Before the guards pounced, a bolt of lightning struck the statue. The marble exploded, sending large pieces of rubble tumbling into the river.

A fierce gust ripped into the crowd, knocking everyone over into the mud. The lashing wind yanked at their robes, tearing the masks off their faces.

The guards lowered their spears and looked upon each other, shrieking as they stumbled backward.

Every face had been purple and scarred and deformed in ways that were wholly unique to them.

The people screamed and clawed at the mud and their own deformed faces as if uncovering some terrible truth. A perpetual lie made divine.

Kiyana smiled; everyone was purple and as ugly as her. No, she thought. They were all as beautiful. She embraced the child and handed her the empty pail. "Go ahead and take what you need," she said. "This land belongs to everyone."

After a moment of dread and loathing, the people slowly stood and composed themselves and for the first time in a long time, they beheld one another as they truly were.

The Night Cyclist

by J. Agombar

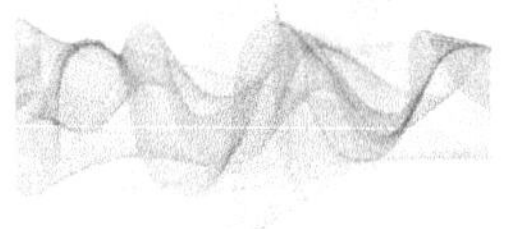

My coffee steams into the crisp midnight air as I glance upon the sparkling stars from my balcony. Living on the coast of Blavega is an experience full of wonder and magic. However, it can get crowded at this time of year with tourists which is why my balcony becomes my retreat. On the night of every November 9th, a grand race is held along Blavega's cobbled coastline road, a twenty-eight-kilometre track that connects the top of Mount Cartlin to the peninsula of the Old Town where I reside.

It calls to celebrate the world of cyclists that gather here, but this event serves merely as a facade for some, for the cobbled road is now twinned with a smoother modern cycle path and few cyclists actually consider it a 'race'.

Nobody rushes this stretch where the coastal breeze changes the banal feeling of just existing into something more, a euphoric higher plane where the gulls above observe, matching the speed of even the more agile riders. The biggest secret is the least mentioned in advertising, but the most talked about in the town. The masses come in an attempt to catch a glimpse of the 'night cyclist', a spirit that can be found on rare occasions, and even rarer, an encounter with a strange illusion where the rider is momentarily transported to another place.

I have been lucky. In my experience, he can only be found on certain nights when the moon is full and only reveals himself to a certain kind of person. Having lived here for several years, and initially not aware of this phantom cyclist, it so happens he was always more likely to reveal himself to someone like me.

Each year after the event, I find tourists and locals in café's and bars garrulous about their experience, flaunting some fanciful story as to how they were briefly haunted by the fearsome spirit world. But these stories are fabricated, mere poetics to impress the guileless masses who pass on the tale in a chain of whispers, a desperate grasp for attention.

The genuine ones are different. I know how they react, more subtle in their approach to the description. They are reserved, confused, and hesitant to reveal due to not expecting to witness such a strange occurrence. Some are lost in translation if their English is not so strong. But certain elements of what they say make it seem natural. Certain perceptive intricacies concrete the validity of their experience. Firstly, they take the time, usually alone, to think about what they saw and ponder if reality had taken them away briefly, or perhaps if an overactive imagination had temporarily overcome them. Then they look around the bar, or coffee shop, not quite knowing who to tell, for they want someone who already knows to assure them, to put their mind at ease, to let them know if they were actually just dreaming.

When I first moved here a few years ago in the height of autumn, my oblivion to such a graceful spirit was resolved by an old local man who had been climbing Blavega's steep inclines since his childhood. He was drunk, and initially, I cast his tales aside before heading home.

Then, after hearing about him. I was compelled and went looking for the spirit. That is how I learned that actively seeking him will always end fruitless. A year passed and another invasion of crimson and ochre leaves fell to the cobblestones.

I'd forgotten all about him until one September evening when the twilight battled with the antique streetlamps. I saw him or saw something. I had ridden less than five kilometers leisurely and free of expectation, a classic trigger for his appearance. As I pulled up to where a low sea wall framed the last glimpse of the sunset, I stopped and released my drink from the bottle cage on the frame beneath me. A meek current of air, a slight zephyr, pushed across behind me. I turned my head to see him as he passed. His brown jacket and flat cap were what I noticed first. He half turned as he rode away, slightly tipping it to greet me, or so I believe. The bike was an odd shape which caused my main confusion at the sight of him, but as I completed my journey home that day I realized exactly whom I had seen and finally felt a sense of belonging in the town I still call home today.

Over a period of time, I saw him sporadically from a distance, sometimes even from my balcony here. The visions were fleeting and barely noticeable, like passing through smoke only to find it disappearing as you disturb it. Around three months ago was my longest and most profound experience of him.

During a cycle home just before dusk, I had stopped for breath moments from my home. The rain had fallen lightly for some time and scattered dark clouds blocked the last remaining light that shone behind them. It caused them to glow at the edges and a rainbow formed in the distance. It was the worst few days of summer weather that followed a heatwave.

Of course, I wasn't prepared for this weather, and my hair became soaked to my head. However, as I ducked for shelter under the canopy of a local baker's shop which was closed, I noticed a man standing by the low sea wall, staring out to sea.

I knew who he was immediately as it was too strange for anybody to be left on the coastal road in the rain, except for the odd tourist, perhaps.

I watched him oversee the rippling bay for a moment before he moved and retrieved a bike that was not present, yet somehow leaned against the nearby lamppost. Like him and his bike, the lamppost also shimmered in the light like a prism turning and glinting. As he mounted it, it presented my weary vision with a blurry motion. He cocked his leg over the sturdy frame and rode away.

I wasn't an expert in bikes, but I knew my way around one. I had not seen the type he had before, but I knew it was not from this modern age, and likely a relic of the past. I later researched the frame style. It was a Hercules, trade bicycle that had a wider frame than usual with a kink in it so you could hang an advertisement board within it. There was also a basket frame below the handlebars. I didn't get much more from that moment, so I took a chance on getting a cold, jumped on my uncouth modern Ammaco Ethos mountain bike, and followed him, taking me towards Mount Cartlin and away from home.

I knew eagerness would likely collapse the vision, so I calmly kept my distance. He seemed to follow the path of the cobblestones but found no friction from them, whereas I stuck to the modern cycle path that ran alongside them.

As I trailed behind him attempting to catch a closer glimpse of his bike, I felt a strange sensation. My body became numb, and the rain stopped. I felt heat as the temperature seemed to rise rapidly around me. The sun burst out from behind the clouds, and the sky turned a bright blue with daylight once more.

The ground in front of me unfolded differently. As I approached him I slowed to stay in his wake. Vibrant colors burst from the ground and everything around me, dancing with incendiary motion. It was like the rippling effect a boat leaves on the water behind it but thickly applied like the strokes of a pastiche painting. Each color matched its component: the cobblestones, a grey and auburn; the ocean, a lazuline blue; the shop window frames of umber and yellow, and the grass on the richer side of

Mount Cartlin a sensational green. Everything became a visual fantasy in lucid and eidetic form.

The colors then blended with their opposing tones with dark blues, violets, and browns that transcended into an otherworldly nighttime. It injected a curious feeling of warmth and freedom into my mind as well as my body. I could no longer feel the aches of the day, nor the rain which had drenched me.

I continued my pursuit with lungs expanding to their full capacity and entranced by the imagery of another era that quivered before me. I gained a little momentum as I let the apparition take me on his beauteous journey toward the mountain.

Suddenly, the smell of bread filled my nostrils, strong and fresh. It became hard to see him in that moment of pace, but his basket under his handlebars contained two loaves stacked in an equanimous fashion and separated with some apples. Although his attire was not a uniform, it was smart enough to warrant an occupation of some kind. His build was that of a regular working class man and not the modern lycra lathered, agile visitors who crossed the same stones each year.

I noticed his front wheel was slightly smaller than the rear, although his tires seemed to be smooth, motionless circles in this strange parallel void, and his spokes near invisible. An array of souls, bursting with stop-motion color appeared around us and seemed to acknowledge him. A woman in a red coat waved a gloved hand at him, a small dog yanked at his master's lead to chase the wheels, and he swerved a little to avoid the football of a young boy who darted across the promenade.

I marveled at the shifting dark hues of the blue sky above which allowed the stars to glint with spectral, momentary beauty. I felt like my eyes were a prisoner of Van Gogh, and as I glanced at my own body I found it had succumbed to the same artistic layered style the world around me had taken. Lines of flickering light blended with thick daubs of color which flaked away from my hands and shirt as my bike cut through the backwash of the unreal cyclist ahead of me.

My journey ended as he pulled over to a place just before the mountain. An old house with brown and red paneling where the windows were grilled with steel diamond emblems and lined with flowers. He slowed and leaned his bike against another lamppost. He then gathered the bread and apples from the basket and glanced up at the house. A woman emerged from the double doors and onto the balcony. She wore a long stylish mauve coat with high heels and a dark hat with a face veil. She smiled and blew him a kiss. I could see the cyclist's face clearly for the first time, a long, thin face and sturdy jaw with dark eyebrows against pale skin, although in reaction to her, he adopted a florid expression and broad smile.

The lady above retired into her house, leaving the balcony doors open. He stopped and looked at me. I froze. He sustained his broad grin, added a wink, and tossed me an apple. I instinctively went to catch it and did successfully as it swirled and resonated with restless sanguine shades in my palm. I snapped my head back up to him in bewilderment where his form lost its colorful shimmering flair and became a more ghostly transparent outline as he passed through the closed doorway of the house, and disappeared. The balcony door above was then closed, or perhaps in this moment of time, never opened. The vision faded, as did the bike against the lamppost, and I was left alone once more in the light rain of that evening.

So, I no longer strive to see the phantom the other cyclists speak of. They say the spirit of the night cyclist haunts this place as if with vendetta or malice, wandering lost with some developed torment. Yet they still seek him, wanting to believe in their own mindless folklore. My heuristic approach has taught me otherwise. To me, the night cyclist represents the opposite nature. He is a happy soul, and appears before those who achieve that same mindful clarity, free of judgment and stressful acquirement. To me, he is the soul of a blessed man, a man in love with all aspects that he surrounds himself with, a rarity to be envied by many, and indeed, the soul of this very town.

Father and the Crows

by Zoltan Komer

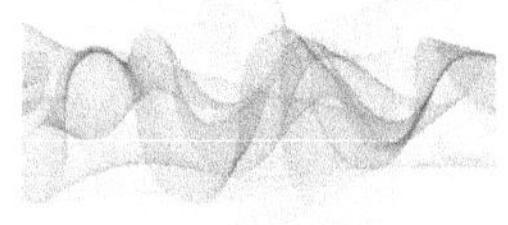

*T*he birds must be frightened away, son— was the only instruction father gave me after he nailed me to the cross in the middle of the yellow field. Around me, there was dry corn everywhere. From time to time, the breeze would blow, and cracking stalks reminded me of a collapsing hovel. The spirits of long-gone scarecrows chasing each other playfully behind the rows.

"Soon you can join us, boy!" They whispered and laughed, dancing around me as I hung on that cross, nailed to the wood, rose petals flopping out of my wounds.

Sometimes, Mother visited me with a jug of water. She was a dear woman.

"Your father makes you work so hard, but you are such a good boy," said Mother, and she always went back to the house with tears on her face, while I scolded myself because I didn't say a word while she was there. Of course, what could I say to her? I was on the edge of my strength. At least, as a silly little boy, that's what I thought, and

I wanted to save my last words for Father: "Dad! I didn't see any birds! Not even one!"

Dad never visited me. He must have thought I was doing a good job. I stayed where he hanged me, frightening the birds away with my young glance, just fine.

I really don't remember how many days I spent on that dilapidated cross. My back was full of splinters, jammed deep into my skin—a big heap of rose petals accumulating under me, which now I could reach with my bare feet. I just kicked them into the corn and loved how I could paint the yellow corn into red. I was doing this when finally, my mother came for me—her skirt floating around her as she ran—and she pulled the nails out of my hands.

"Your father is dead!" She yelled.

I barely understood the meaning of her words. I felt really dizzy after those hot summer days on the cross, not to mention the lonely nights. But after a few moments, I finally realized what she was saying.

Dad? He is dead?

Pulling myself together, I ran into the house, side by side with Mother. And there he was. He lay in the bed. As I got closer, I realized it wasn't him at all. It was just an old scarecrow wearing my father's blue pajama trousers.

"He's dead," whispered Mother, putting her white hand on my shaking shoulder. The rose petals were falling from my wounded palm, slowly covering the floor.

First I saw some movement from the corner of my eye, a gathering of small black bodies in the window, and when I turned my head towards them the crows let out their sharp voices. "Caw, caw!"

"Mother, the birds are here!" I screamed, but it was too late to do anything about it, and even a closed window couldn't stop these birds; there were hundreds of them. They flooded into the room and covered the thin body of my father. They stabbed their beaks into his chest and started to pull out straw filaments. I ran to the bed and started weaving my small hands because the birds must be frightened away, as Father once said, but my childish efforts were useless: Dad disappeared in a moment.

Only a pair of blue pajama trousers was left of him. A rag, something that housewives use for scrubbing the tile floor, and I remember, after a few years, my mother used it just for that. I'd catch her crying. She didn't know, didn't suspect, I was watching her. Blue rose petals escaped from her eyes and slowly fell on the floor, but in a moment, just like she was trying to hide some kind of evidence, she immediately smeared her tears with that dirty-looking, torn rag.

The Feast

by Miriam H. Harrison

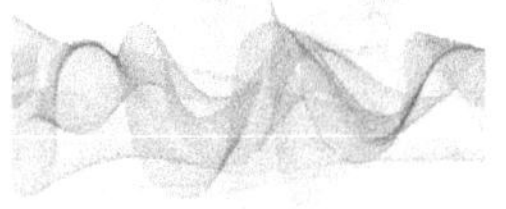

There would be bodies. Her mother had already warned her about the smell, about the morbid pull of curiosity. *You'll want to look,* she had said. *But don't. You'll only spoil your appetite.*

In her unease, Isa had no appetite left to spoil. She paddled through the darkness, having only old habits to guide her. There was nothing to see but blackness, nothing to hear but the whispering waters against her paddle. She tried to remember her mother's words, the pieces of advice scattered like breadcrumbs to lead her home.

They want you to believe you don't belong here. They think your humanity will make you weak, but you can prove them wrong. You will show them you belong.

Belong. It was a strange word—one that never seemed to fit. Did she ever truly belong here among the shapeshifters and specters? Here where the river was dark with spirits and the sun was an unconvincing myth? Those whispers from the water echoed her doubts, but there among the murmurs was another voice, clearer in its familiarity.

They want you to doubt. They want your questions to shake you. They want you to believe you belong to a world you have never seen. But this is your home to claim—if you want it.

Wanting was a luxury Isa had never known, though it had built her world. Wanting had driven her mother to the under realm, driven her to eat their dark feast and trade sunlight for shadows. Isa had been born into these shadows, born of flesh fed by the under realm. For a time, that had been enough to claim her place. But that time had passed with her mother. Her mother's wanting had brought them here; her heart and passion had made it home. But Isa did not have her heart. Without its steady rhythm, could any place be home?

Faint torchlight flickered far across the water. Isa paddled closer, drawn to the light like the many crawling, scuttling things of the deep. She could sense their movements in the cavern around her. As the light grew stronger, she could see the dark shapes, moving along the walls and ceiling, their bodies long as her canoe, their legs, eyes, and carapaces gleaming.

At last, Isa drew up close to the rocky shore. She pulled her vessel safely up from the whispering waters, away from the paths of hurrying insects. They had cleared trails through the dirt, the torchlight drawing them to earthen tunnels that glowed with a still deeper light.

This was as far as Isa had ever come. Every other year she had sat with the canoe as her mother changed for the feast, disappearing among the swarm. She only knew the feast as a time of boredom and waiting. But not this year.

Isa followed the eager procession of insects, jostled by their long bodies through too-narrow tunnels until at last, they emerged into a wide cavern. Here, the polished stone walls gleamed in the glow of countless torches, illuminating a seething heap at the centre of the chamber that rose high above her. The insects hurried into this heap, hungry for the feast, the air above them filled with warm light and the stench of decay.

You came.

Isa looked up high to the top of the writhing heap. There, atop a tower of bones stripped bare by the frenzy, sat two great beetles. One, purple black, was feeding on the maggots born of the heap. Beside him, his queen gleamed in emerald tones. She watched Isa, her gaze steady over twitching antennae.

"Yes, your Highness," Isa said, quickly dropping into a low bow. "I have come to join the feast."

Why?

Isa looked up into those emerald eyes. Under their gaze, her answers suddenly felt fragile, empty.

"This is my home," she said at last. "I wish to stay."

Why?

Isa's tongue sat empty. She thought only of the whispering river, the voice that carried above all others, speaking in death with more heart and strength than Isa had ever felt in life.

"This is my home," she said again. "This is the world my mother chose. I choose it, too."

The emerald queen considered her in silence. Then as Isa watched, those insect features melted, twisted, and shaped themselves into a new form. Isa looked up into a human face, beautiful and tragic.

"I know of the choice between worlds," the queen said. "I know of the strength of mothers, too—how they can tie you to a world of their choosing. But what of your strength?"

Looking into the queen's face, Isa thought of her mother's features, her strength. Isa had inherited her eyes, and her nose, when what she needed most was her heart.

"My strength is my choice," Isa said. "I choose to stay."

"Then eat."

At the queen's words, a path cleared through the heap's frenzy. The bodies of countless dead creatures were exposed—raw and rotten—and despite her mother's warning, Isa looked. There in the heap was a familiar form with eyes and nose much like her own, though bloated with death and decay.

You'll only spoil your appetite.

Despite the grief and revulsion churning her stomach, Isa stepped forward. She climbed into the heap, the way wet and slippery with death, but she continued until she reached her mother's body. Much of her torso had already been eaten away, but her ribcage was intact, its strength guarding her great treasure.

You will show them you belong.

Isa reached into her mother's chest and pulled from it her heart. It filled her hand, heavy and still. Could this thing be the same heart that had brought her mother to this place, that had brought Isa to this moment?

She bit into it.

Isa's mouth filled with a warm wetness, with the taste and smell of rot. But as she ate, her senses changed. Each bite became sweeter, more satisfying, tasting of pomegranates. That taste fed a deep hunger that had gone unnamed. It was an awakening—the answer to questions she had never thought to ask.

Fed by her mother's flesh, a new strength flowed through her. It sprang from her own heart, reaching out into the many limbs that stretched from her newly formed body. That strength surrounded her, joining her in the frenzy all around. Her senses filled with life, with connection, with the thrill of the feast.

She ate, savoring the sweetness of home.

Of the Stars

by Miriam H. Harrison

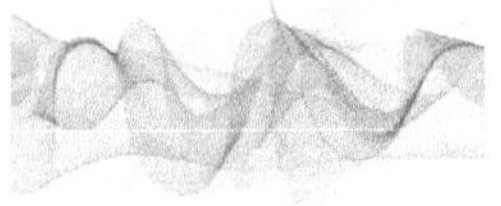

For as long as she could remember, Emma had looked to the stars. They were her one promise of perfection glittering high above the rest of her life. Her favorite memories were of sneaking out at night while camping with her family. It was a short walk from the cabin door down to the dock that stretched out into the small lake, and no matter how dark the night was, her feet could always find their way over the worn pebble path.

From the end of the dock, it seemed that the whole world was stars. A still night was best; with the water calm and smooth, she had stars below and stars above, with only the serrated line of pines cutting the worlds in two. Emma wished that she could climb above that jagged edge to where the stars were brightest.

Emma tried to carry those stars with her wherever she went. When she closed her eyes, she could still see them there, winking secretly behind her eyelids. She kept that image with her as a close companion when her family would bring her back to town. The sun was never too bright for her to find her stars.

Emma was almost twelve when she learned that she wouldn't be going back to the camp. No one else in her family seemed to notice the loss. Talk of divorce filled everyone's mouth, leaving room for little else but tears and anger. Alone, Emma mourned the stars.

On clear nights she would peer out her window and count what stars she could find. There were always a few to greet her, but never enough to fill her growing emptiness. She closed her eyes and returned to the ones she kept hidden inside. They glittered and gleamed, and as she spent more time with them, they began to glow more brightly.

It wasn't long before Emma spent most of her time behind her eyes. If her family worried about her time alone, they didn't show it. In fact, it was only when her vision started to fade that they took notice at all.

At first, it seemed to be a minor concern. Emma made a trip to the optometrist and came home with a pair of glasses. Her family was satisfied. They returned to their shouting, and she returned to her stars. But when she woke the next morning and put on her glasses, her eyesight was even worse. By the time she was taken to a doctor, the world around her was little more than shadows, scattered with her stars. The doctors and specialists could offer no explanation.

Her parents had new things to cry and scream about, but Emma was at peace. She had lost her sight, but kept her stars. She felt for the first time how pointless all the rest was. Fleeting details, distractions. There among the stars, she felt a surer sense of being, of permanence. Maybe that's all eternity was: stars and light and beauty.

Over time, she became aware of a constant hum, an indiscernible undertone to the sounds around her. It was only when it grew louder that Emma matched its tones to the pulse and twinkle of the stars. She listened closely and heard their voices. The stars sang of all they had seen. They sang of hopes, promises, and loss. They were sad, beautiful songs of the worlds beneath their watch. Always they sang, and always there were new songs to be sung.

Emma fell in love with the music. For a time, she could hear the fear and anger of her parents over the gentle voices, but despite the work of doctors and surgeons, even that faded away. She felt the fullness of the songs within her, a deeper rhythm that held the pace of eternity. She noticed from time to time that the bed beneath her had become a constant presence, but what did that matter? How could anything beyond the stars and their melody matter?

The pulse of the music moved more deeply inside her until she couldn't help but dance. It wasn't long before hands stopped her, and strapped her down. They couldn't hear the music, and she couldn't explain. Still, she followed the songs. Any part of her that could move tapped and swayed. She felt the music. She was the music.

As she danced her half-dance, a new light grew. Emma saw her body glow, dimly at first and then brighter and brighter with each new song. She now felt the lyrics gathering on her tongue, and as she opened her mouth to sing, she felt the bed and its world slip away. She let it go and joined in the perfection of the stars.

Big Sis

by Madeleine McDonald

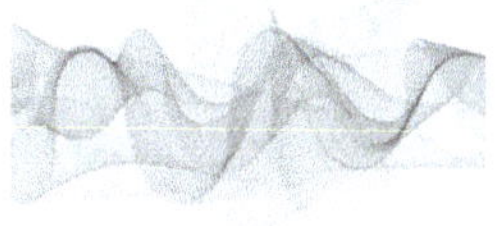

I took the tablets ten minutes ago. It took longer than I thought to swallow the whole packet, even though I made cocoa with extra sugar to remove the bitter taste.

They won't work yet, I know.

I lie in bed, eyes closed, wondering what the real dark will feel like. It's never properly dark in our bedroom because of the streetlamps. Lisa is out there, in the real dark, and it's my job to find her. No one else can do it.

The house feels empty without her. She was always banging and crashing and dropping things. "Butterfingers," Dad called it, but he ruffled her hair when he said it. Dyspraxia, the doctors call it. We know a lot of medical words in our house.

Right now, even without the little noises of Lisa grunting and breathing in the next bed, I feel fuzzy and warm. And safe. Mom has gone to bed, and Dad is splashing in the bathroom. I know it's Dad because he sings old pop songs in the bath. At least he doesn't sing in public. Darren is still up, watching television downstairs. I can hear gunfire, explosions, and car chase music, so he's probably watching an old James Bond movie. The house is settling down for the night around us, and the heating pipes clank as they cool down.

Lisa is out there, in the dark, missing this cocoon of safety.

I hear water now. Soft splashing that underpins Dad's vigorous splashing in the bathroom next door. Then a pattering of rain on the window. Have you ever noticed that water is never still? It always wants to go somewhere else. That's a scientific fact. Even trapped in a glass, it won't stay still. It took Lisa a long time to learn how to balance a cup without spilling some.

The water lifts me. My bed becomes a raft. The raft bears me away, gently, so gently. With my eyes closed, I hear the tiny eddies it leaves in its wake. The river is broad, somehow I sense that, and the current runs smoothly. My raft is warm and safe above the dark water.

When we were little, we told each other the clanking radiator was saying goodnight. We called the one in our room Ernesto. I forget why now. He was just included in the roll call of toys we said goodnight to. The ones in our beds, and the ones up on the shelf. It took us a long time to lie there and say goodnight to all of them by name.

Sometimes I wanted to go to sleep quickly, but I couldn't because Lisa insisted on saying her goodnights. Even with the lights out, I could imagine her mulish expression. Whenever things didn't go Lisa's way, she put on what Dad called her busy-Lizzie face. She used to fold her arms across her chest, pout, and refuse to do what people asked. She understood what they wanted her to do, like she understood I wanted to go to sleep, but she wasn't interested in how other people felt. That's the way Lisa was.

Dad could usually coax her out of it. Our teachers used to roll their eyes and put on a fake cajoling voice to talk her out of her strop. I hated people talking to her differently. To me, she was just Lisa, my little sister, ten minutes younger than me. I'm her interpreter, and I've been responsible for her since we began to walk and talk.

She was born different. "Like some people are born with blue eyes and some with brown," Mom explained. "It's genetic. It's nothing to do with being a twin." I remember her sad smile. "It's nothing to do with anything. It just happened."

A new boy at school once said, "Your sister is an ugly dwarf." I kicked him hard on the leg, and he never said it again. I wish I could do the same to Facebook trolls now. His mom complained, and

I heard Mum tell a neighbor, "I gave her short shrift." I didn't know what the words meant then.

I like hearing new words. I save them up to use them in the right place. I like seeing the surprise on grown-ups' faces when I use a difficult word. I wonder if there will be words in the dark. Then I tell myself, of course, there will; otherwise, I won't be able to talk to Lisa and reassure her. I've always been there for her. I'm Big Sis.

I know a lot more words than Lisa does. That's not just because I'm ten minutes older. Cognitive delay is another term I heard doctors using. Mum and Dad insisted she could go to primary school along with me, but she fell further and further behind. Then we moved to a new house, so she could attend a special school.

We buried Lisa in her favorite dress, the one with red and blue spots, although it had become too tight for her. Delayed puberty, the doctor said. Me, I started my periods two years ago. Lisa put on weight, and she complained bras were uncomfortable and kept pulling hers off, or else she cut them up and hid them. In the end, Mom gave in and let her not wear one.

In the dark, other people won't be able to see her, or her Facebook pictures, so they can't make spiteful comments on her weight or her appearance. I will hold her hand, and she will know Big Sis is there.

We used to go for Sunday walks by the river because it was somewhere safe for Lisa. The waiter ignored us, busy going somewhere else. After rain, the level rose, and it flowed with purpose, with leaves and small logs bobbing on its surface.

The water beneath my raft flows with purpose now. I think that means the tablets are beginning to work. I paid a boy called Andy $20 to steal a packet of his mom's sleeping tablets. She's an alcoholic, and he said she wouldn't notice straight away. I couldn't even pronounce the complicated name on the packet, but I could read most of the leaflet inside, so I knew he didn't cheat me.

The raft spins. The water beneath me flows faster. I open my eyes and try to raise my head off the pillow. My muscles won't obey, and I can't see in the murk. I call to Lisa.

Is that her answering call? I think so, but the water is loud and angry. The dark enfolds me, thick and dense. It fills my eyes, nose, and mouth. It tastes woolly like I'm chewing on knitting, but not in an uncomfortable way. I try to raise my right hand to see if I can make out the fingers, but my arm lies inert. Beepo is tucked safely under my left arm. We buried Lisa with her favourite toy, Dan-dan, so it's only fair that I get to bring Beepo.

The four of us will be together.

I won't see tomorrow's daylight peeping through the curtains. I won't hear the house waking up. None of that matters.

"I'm here, Lisa. Hold tight to Dan-dan. Me and Beepo are coming."

The river is in spate now. I can't hear Lisa's reply.

The roaring ahead is louder. The raft tilts at a crazy angle. I'm sliding, reaching for Lisa's hand.

The dark embraces us both.

OAK AND LINDEN

by Madeleine McDonald

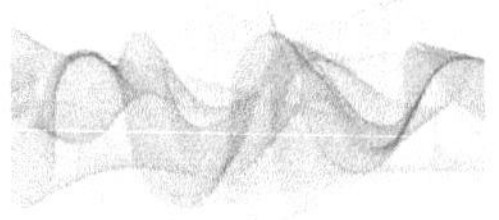

Isn't that just typical of men! Neither of them asked *me* what I wanted.

I had been uneasy all evening. Something was not right. Phil's old mate Zooey turned up at the door late one afternoon. They hugged, danced around the hall, and hugged again before either of them spared me a glance.

Then Phil drew me in. "Hey, Zooey, meet Barb, the love of my life." As always, I heard the note of pride in his voice. "What I did to deserve such a wonderful woman, I don't know."

Zooey nodded politely. Phil chattered on. "Zooey and I were in my first band, at school. He was the drummer. Can you imagine? We practiced in Ben's dad's garage."

"Until Ben failed his math A level."

They crowed with laughter.

"Poor Ben. His mom put him under house arrest for the summer."

"Yeah, he was pig sick to miss our first gig."

"In that bikers' pub."

"Real hard men, they were. And we didn't realize till we got there they were all gay!"

More crows of laughter. Phil and Zooey disappeared into the kitchen to help themselves to cans of beer and took their drinks to the conservatory.

I was pleased to see Phil enjoying himself, but they were so busy talking that they more or less ignored me for the rest of the evening.

Well, not quite. Zooey said nothing out of place. I told myself I was imagining things when I sensed the occasional lecherous look in my direction. The hairs on my neck rose but he smoothed the lechery off his face before I even turned round, leaving only a cheery smile. Yet something lingered in the air. I didn't trust him.

What I did not imagine was the duck. I brought mugs of coffee into the conservatory and Phil made some room by sweeping a pile of newspapers aside. Albert fell to the floor. The tray slipped from my hands, and I burst into tears.

"'Never mind love. Accidents happen."

"But it's Albert!" I was on my knees in a puddle of coffee, holding pieces of Albert. Even superglue would not put him back together again.

So silly to make a spectacle of myself over a pottery ornament. I put the pieces on the tray and went to the kitchen to find a cloth. Behind me, I heard Phil's hissed explanation to Zooey. "It's the change of life. Barb's been taking things to heart lately."

Lightning flashed in the gathering gloom. Thunder rattled the windows. When I brought a cloth and bucket into the conservatory, Albert was sitting on top of the pile of newspapers, intact.

"No harm done. At least it wasn't the duck," Phil remarked to Zooey. "Hideous little fellow, isn't he? We bought him on honeymoon, as a joke, but he came with us into our first home, and we've cherished him ever since." He patted Albert on the head. "He's been with us through thick and thin, hasn't he, Barb?"

So, Phil remembered too. We had parked the camper van in a nondescript little town, somewhere in Belgium. It was raining that day but the future lay golden before us. When Phil spotted a comical pottery duck on a market stall and joked that it would make a good souvenir of our rain-soaked honeymoon, the sun came out in my heart. The purchase made, we feasted on those succulent Belgian fries with mayonnaise in a cafe called *Chez Albert.* Before we set off again, I had wrapped Albert the duck in layers of T-shirts to protect him from damage.

On my knees on the tiled floor of the conservatory, I mopped the puddle of coffee dry and put the cloth in the bucket. *Phil, you were there, you saw Albert hurtle to the floor and shatter. Why are you acting as if nothing happened?*

Rain hammered on the conservatory roof. Zooey stroked Albert's orange beak with one finger. "Maybe he wants to go for a swim on the lawn."

Is that supposed to be funny? But Phil doubled over with laughter, and I moved Albert to safety.

I did not imagine it. I did not. Back in the kitchen, breathing hard, I slowly repeated the words. I was not going to question my own sanity. I hated it when Phil blamed everything on menopause. For a lovely, caring man, he had a blind spot about *The Change.* He seemed to think rubbing my back and murmuring, "You'll always be beautiful to me, Barb," would somehow magic away hot flashes and mood swings.

When I took mugs out of the cupboard to make fresh coffee, I left a tiny smear of blood from where a splinter of pottery had pierced my thumb.

I made sandwiches and left them to reminisce. Phil's bid for rock stardom had not outlasted his university years. Instead, he earned a precarious living as a freelance session musician. We had never been rich, but if Phil was happy, I was happy.

Zooey dismissed his own career as, "This and that, you know, moving and shaking." However, he had made a pile of money, if the B.M.W. parked outside was anything to go by. I wondered if the single earring was a real diamond.

Eventually, he took his leave. I stood back in case he tried to embrace me; instead, he kissed my hand. "My dear Barb, it has been an honor to meet you." He mock punched Phil on the arm. "Our Phil picked a good 'un when he met you."

I managed a smile.

"Hey, you two, answer me this. If you could make just one wish, what would it be?"

To see you walk out the door and never come back.

Phil put his arm around my shoulders. "One wish? You know what, Zooey and I say this most sincerely. I want us to die together. That I shall not weep by her grave, nor she by mine."

Good God, he's drunk, quoting poetry. I'll have to get him to bed.

"It shall be done."

His voice was thunder. Lightning bathed us but did not burn. My bare feet sank through the hall carpet and through the floorboards, seeking the comfort of damp earth. Roots thickened, holding me tall and proud. Tendrils sprang from my toes to race through the soil. Blood and bone, skin and sinew dissolved, replaced by a lattice of simple cells. Rough bark protected me. The hot pulse of blood was replaced by the creep of sap.

My transient irritation with Phil vanished. His hand on my shoulder became the scrape of branches entangled with mine. Phil, the backbone of my life, was there still.

Under the starlit sky, Zooey extended his hands over us in blessing.

Typical men. Neither of them asked me what I wanted. However, now I've got used to it, I have no objections to living as a tree. I like my sturdy, serene existence. Birdsong soothes me. Each year, my roots anchor me deeper as I wait for my green mantle to unfurl again, for the creep of sap that urges me sunwards, tall and proud.

Our grandchildren bring their children here, to play under our shared canopy, and collect acorns to plant. I hear them telling the story of how, on this very spot, an isolated house was struck by lightning and burned to the ground. "Phil and Barb's spirits are here, in the place they loved," they tell the little ones. "Look how the two trees have grown into each other, on the very spot where the house once stood. Oak and linden, interwoven." They smile at each other over the children's heads, disbelieving their own words, retelling a fairy tale once told to them as children.

Indeed, I look forward to hundreds of years beside my beloved Phil. Zooey did grant us that.

But, and this is a big but, I liked our life the way it was. Why did it have to end so abruptly? We had a dolphin-watching holiday in Cornwall booked for that summer, and I had promised Phil new binoculars for his birthday. Why couldn't Zooey, keeper of the thunder, have shown himself magnanimous, and allowed us to marvel at cavorting dolphins before he granted Phil's wish? I would have died happy after seeing them leap and plunge.

Not to mention that I never replied to that email from my cousin in New Zealand and left a thousand other things undone.

Men! They make these big romantic gestures, and they forget it's the little connections we women make that keep the world turning.

Still, you can't have everything. All in all, I am content. When the wind blows, his leaves tickle mine. I like that. It reminds me of the way we slept in our human form. He threw an arm over my shoulder, trapping me under his protection, and snuggled into my back. His snuffles caressed the nape of my neck all night.

When the wind blows, it sharpens my memories, and my leaves tickle his.

The Many-Colored Star

by Sam M. Phillips

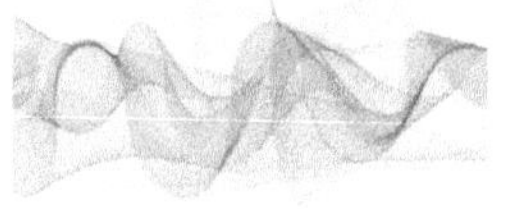

The greenhouse on the hill has become an angry place for me. I need to walk away. So, I do, get out of the place for a while, a short step to precede the long one; I'll be moving out soon. Down the hill I go, frustrated and annoyed. Family—the loved ones pulled too close—who can fathom them?

My nephew—five and scattered like the wind—has been annoying all day today; constant nonsensical babble dribbling from his twirling head as he spins around. Who can stand it? My brother doesn't pull him into line, and my mother is too afraid to be the ogre. It isn't my place.

I feel for the kid, but I want to throttle him. Hours and hours of it; the never ceasing talking. Talking about nothing, to no one. What planet is he on? Aren't I strange enough? Do we really need another one?

My parents and I have been arguing. It never really ceases these days. They want me on medication. I don't want to go on medication. They are stubborn and so am I: an impasse. There is more but it is too complicated to explain.

Besides, I too seek escape, even now, so the walking must commence, the long walk away. Oh well, life is full of such cycles, of the death and the rebirth, of the existence apparent in the transformation from one to the other.

The sun is still up, and it is dominating. I wear my strange hat; there is no describing it. I refuse. My other clothes are not so sacred, the red board shorts, the black sneakers, the white seventies style exercise singlet with its non-synthetic cotton and blue trim. I wear my sunglasses as always, my phone in my pocket.

Through the village I go. A suburb locked away in the sugar cane, a little retreat from reality, where people come to escape their lives, or else to live them, it is impossible to tell. It is so dull—perhaps peaceful—here. It is certainly beautiful, with the neat lawns and the trees, and the huge expanse of blue sky, stretching off into forever.

Forever, I'm lost. It's been going on forever. Why can't I be different? There's no real need; I just want to stop hurting people. Just being alive seems to hurt everyone. Perhaps I'm just melodramatic, I certainly am restless enough. I certainly seem to stir up trouble in people. Others I calm, but you can't calm family. Family is drama.

So, I take note of myself and my feelings and thoughts; perhaps they'll make a good story when I get home. Perhaps I'll actually have the energy and drive to commit this moment to paper. One day you shall read it. How far from now? The distance seems unbearable.

A long way from home now, walking in the sugar cane fields. They sway, green and majestic. An endless expanse, symbolic of something indescribable. I kick the dirt, wondering why I'm even looking down. What is that? I go back— nothing—a rock. I keep walking. It happens again and again. Oh my god, it's starting.

Ignore it, keep walking. I'm out to make a call. Why is there no reception at home, yet here, not so far away really, there is? What's so special about this place? I'm hidden in the green and brown world of the field now, in the shadow of the growing crop, hidden from the road and the cars full of eyes.

She has been texting me. I want to talk to her. It makes me happy. I must wait. From somewhere, a tone will sound and give me the signal I desire. It is time. I ring.

On the phone now and forever; at least, I want it to last forever. She and I lost in our world together, wrapped up in one another. We talk of truths and fantasies, dreams and realities. It is sobering and magical, dancing on a knife's edge. I feel truly alive to hear her voice, the whole universe contracts, and the moments slow and become omnipotent.

This is my point; every story has a point. It isn't just a random event, or some nonsense tale with a beginning, middle, and end. True stories have a message, a reason. Here is mine.

The sun has gone down; I am walking home in the dark. I am distracted by many different shapes. My obsessive-compulsive disorder sends me back to check them, annoying in the dark. I want to be home; it is cold and windy, my head stuffed with moldy cheese. I have no idea what is wrong with me or what is causing the headaches.

Eventually, I remembered the phone call; what I said to her. This is a moment like no other. There will never be another like it. I must pay attention. I must be alive in the here and now.

I look up. There are many stars in the sky; out in the country they are stark and beautiful gems set in an ink-black sea, but one is more radiant than the others. Straight ahead, as if guiding me home, it dances, the many-colored star. Lightning flash strobe light of green, white, purple, red, blue, orange; it is all and none, everything and one.

It is this moment, and I shall remember it forever.

I Am Home

by Sam M. Phillips

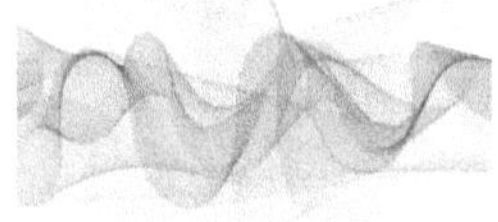

I am home, staring at the wall as I sip my coffee, a lost, tumbling sensation inside me trying to reconcile what I have left behind. There is a hole—a shape so familiar—receding into a background against my wishes. Here the blackness has no edge of hope, and yet there is always hope, for there is always another day, and another chance to be near you once more.

It is nearly impossible to think, the family swirling around me, calling to each other from distant rooms. They are wound up in their monotony and their tasks, their preparations. At least they will be gone soon, and I will be left to my writing—and my memories of you.

Is it only last night that I held you? Time can be so cruel, that it passes so quickly with you, yet drags in your absence. I feel the distance hurts you even more than it does me, for at least I have my writing to return to, these words to hold me in their comforting embrace, a way to cope, if not forget.

I have become so sure of us, and I have seen this reflected in the deep amber pools of your eyes, so wide and hopeful, drawing me in. There is pain in our past, yet all the obstacles have not soured us. We are more intensely in love than ever, and I know this will only grow, and that, eventually, the distance will become unbearable, and we will be unable to stand being apart.

For now, however, I can remember you here, on this page. And there will be something real, something alive, in the remembering.

I wake up nervous, it has been a stressful week, and I feel your absence more keenly than ever. Losing you is not an option and through all our careful negotiations and words of care and hope I feel like all is so tentative, so tenuous. I need something more solid, more physical, and I crave your touch.

You are the same. Through all our closeness I have learned about your passions and your words of fire, and I am learning to regrow after each scouring. These are just your modes of expression and reflect the intensity of your feelings. I drink you in like a heady brew, knowing you are what I need to feel alive.

Unaware of where the day will eventually lead, I go about my normal routine, making tea, cooking breakfast, and checking emails. There is some distant foreknowledge creeping up on me, but it is as hazy as my mind as I fight to clear the morning fog. Memories of all the highs and lows of our week talking on the phone still gather in subconscious pools, beckoning me to dive in, but yet unable, despite their vividness, to provoke me to rash action.

This state of muddled equilibrium cannot last long, and one or more of my drives will soon come to dominate me. I recognize it, knowing it by long association; an urge to love and be loved, and to be loved by you, for you are my destiny, much as I too have tried to deny this.

Suddenly, I am in a frenzy, and the panic sweeps over me before I even realize what is causing it. This will to action is too much for me, and my body is moving before my mind can contemplate. Then I am left dazed by my own thoughts, trying desperately to catch up with a desire that has run on ahead of me.

I have booked the flight, despite any cost, and I will be leaving this afternoon. Now the issue is decided there is some relaxation, for fate has picked me up yet again, and shaken me like the weightless thing that I am. For a moment there I felt I would go mad with the anxiety, the indecision clawing at me, forcing me to act one way and then another. This always happens when I get an idea that I believe is too big for me to act upon. But, as is always the way, in the doing I am set free, knowing that whatever happens is meant to happen and that I am to be swept along with this passion, this passion you invoke in me.

I am uncomfortable with words, or, at least, with words spoken out loud. There is nothing outside me that is not within me, and all I can do is type or move a pen, unable to reconcile this past reality with the present. For me, there is no dialogue between you and me, nothing that means more than what is felt. Nothing needs to be said when the soul is so heavy with true love.

Then there are the words of others. I feel their grubby handprints upon our lives, and I do not wish them to have any power over us, so I do not let them speak. Here we can be free and true, colored by everything we know only within ourselves when we are together as one being. This unity means there is no need for quotations, no need to hear our conversations, for what can be said that we do not already hear in the vibrations of our hearts?

Yet life is not all, or even mostly, these noble stirrings, and there is a practical cause and effect which we must consider, doing our best to steer our lives, or, rather, to dumbly follow after ourselves once an impulse has taken hold. And so, this is what I must do, for there is still so much uncertainty. You do not even know that I have booked the flight, and I do not know how I will reach the airport, or what I shall do once I arrive. There is no reason for me to believe that you will take me in, for your parents are guarded against me, and so it could easily be that I am sweeping only myself off my feet, and dumping myself in a cold and foreign city, exposed to the brutal elements of both nature and lost love.

My pride, as well as my prudence, balks at the idea, but I ring my mother and ask for her to drive me to the airport. To ask for help is to invite ridicule, for assistance comes with the burden of opinion, and unwelcome advice is sure to follow. These are the slings and arrows I do my best to avoid, the reason I have moved away, and sought life out on my own. Sometimes I wonder how you can bear it, living with your parents as you do, knowing this gives them the right to interfere. But still, we do what we must, for we are young and lost, beings of some other impractical realm of feeling, where pragmatism becomes a burden that must be only temporarily shouldered and then hastily cast off. This is what we seek in each other, the beauty of escape, and the soaring hope of love fulfilled.

Of course, my parents say as they must, as I'm sure your parents will too. Their words are only words, and I let them slide off me, possessing enough of my own concerns with my impetuousness without adding to the burden of fear. There are so many things that can go wrong, and yet these are mundane. I have caught a flight before. I have visited you before. Still, there are unknown factors now, and our relationship flutters like a flag in the breeze. Is this why I rush to you now, to be certain, to put you at ease? Or am I full of fear of losing you, and only with this, some grand gesture of love, do I feel I can express myself, words having failed me?

You are certainly surprised. I text you as I wait for my flight at the airport. I would like to call but I need to buffer myself against the possibility of rejection. Perhaps this is unrealistic and reveals the phantom-like nature of all my doubts, for there is no chance you will reject me. You love me, as I love you.

The flight seems long even though it is only a few hours. I still don't know if I will be able to stay with you at the other end or if I will be forced into whatever hasty arrangements I am capable of making for accommodation. I try to put myself at ease; I have come this far, conquered my anxiety to act on the spur of the moment, and I'm sure I am now more flexible than I have been in the past. A drug addiction can steal so much but I am clawing my way back to normalcy, now more confident than ever, clean and sober, a man once more. This is something the old me would have been unable to do, and I take heart in this. Everything will work out, one way or another. Our relationship has overcome so much already, and I feel like fate is on our side despite any difficulties. The proof is in our determination to be together, and the strong bond we cannot deny.

This is never more evident than when we first see each other after a time apart. I am waiting, looking for your car, lost in the sea of people swarming out of the airport. There is confusion and the air is freezing cold. I shiver and sink into myself, guarding the tiny flame of hope that dwells deep in my heart, not letting the icy breeze come close, not letting the ignorant masses see that I am exposed, out on a limb, my future, and my love at stake.

Then, suddenly, you are here. There is a brief glimpse of each other, so happy and alive, and then we are tight in each other's arms, trying to kiss through the smiles. There is an unreality in this moment, as there always is, so blessed to have found the one who completes me. I think of what I would do for you, and it shocks me. Having come this far on hope, I feel like I could go further, and at this moment, I know there is everything we need right here, in each other's arms.

I know I am truly home.

Snow Angels

by Rayne King

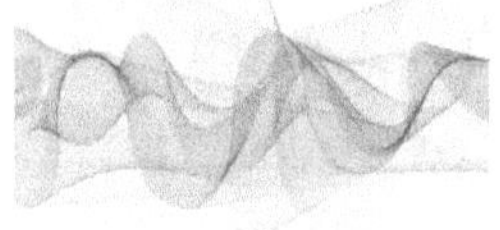

Jocelin and Everly bickered, trading jabs and occasional haymakers. Jocelin guided the family's rundown Subaru wagon along the winding mountainside roads. Nerves ate away at her stomach due to the heavy snowfall. The wagon wasn't as reliable in the winter as it used to be. She'd driven straight home after work and had planned on bunkering down for the night with a couple of generous glasses of cheap red. But as soon as she'd entered the mudroom, her motherly intuition had told her something was amiss. The house had felt empty, lacking her daughter's presence.

Her phone rang.

It had been Everly, asking in an uncharacteristically sheepish voice if Jocelin could come pick her up.

Jocelin had agreed without hesitation. "Where are you?"

". . . at Beau's."

"Not that fucking asshole again! Come on, Ev!"

"Mom. Please, just pick me up," she'd pleaded.

"Jesus Christ," Jocelin spat, retying her snow boots. "I'm on my way." A gust of icy wind rattled the wagon. Jocelin gripped the steering wheel, then dropped the transmission into a lower gear.

Jocelin continued to grill her daughter about the boy she'd been with. "I thought you were done with that little scumbag, anyway?"

"Well, we're done for real now, so don't worry," Everly muttered, staring absently out the passenger window, watching the snowflakes spiral.

The wagon's headlights sliced through the night. The road turned into a wide sweep, running alongside the Ashokan Reservoir.

Squinting through the shrouding darkness, Everly could just make out the frozen surface of the reservoir. The blustery wind kicked up sheets of snow, making it appear as if ghosts were playing around out there.

Suddenly the wagon was sent into a spin, veering off the road. "Shit!" Jocelin cursed, as she realized she'd hit a patch of black ice, hidden beneath the mounting snow. Everly braced herself for possible impact, while Jocelin jerked the wheel back and forth, fighting to return the wagon to the correct direction.

She failed.

The wagon slid onto the shoulder and bumped into a wall of plowed snow that had built up against the guardrail with a bathetic thud.

"Fuck me."

"Nice mouth," Everly teased.

Jocelin sighed. "Not now, Ev."

Shifting into reverse, Jocelin attempted to back up but was unsuccessful as the tires spun on the ice. Growing frustrated, she pushed the gas pedal to the floor, gunning the engine. The smell of burning rubber and clutch stank up the air. Smoke and exhaust billowed out, wafting against the windows, like phantoms seeking refuge.

"We're stuck," Jocelin declared, taking her foot off the gas in acceptance. "Gee, you think?" Everly remarked.

"Lose the goddamn attitude. We're here because of you."

"Don't blame me because you can't drive."

"I'm blaming you because I had to pick your ass up in the middle of a snowstorm." Everly scoffed.

Silence followed.

"Listen, I'm going to get out to push," Jocelin announced. "You get in the driver's seat and keep trying to back up."

"Okay."

"Please don't run me over," Jocelin said, as she clambered out of the car.

"No promises," Everly said, as a sly grin spread across her face.

Jocelin shook her head.

"Mom, this isn't working!" Everly called out.

"We've almost got it," Jocelin answered, lying to both of them. "Let's give it one last try!"

"Okay. . ."

Jocelin dug her boots deeper into the ground and heaved. Everly worked the clutch and revved the engine. Their effort only served to bury the nose of the wagon deeper into the ditch. "Fuck it!" Jocelin snapped, throwing her hands up in defeat. "You're right. It's not working."

"Can't we just call a tow truck or something?" Everly whined.

Jocelin grimaced at the thought of the bill, but couldn't think of any other options. "Looks like we're going to have to at this point."

Withdrawing her phone from her coat pocket, Jocelin was dismayed to see she didn't have any cell service. "I'm not getting any bars," she said.

Everly pulled out her phone, hoping for a different result, but her screen displayed zero bars as well. "Same for me," she said, as she leaned her head out the window.

"Shit," Jocelin hissed. She scanned the surrounding landscape. Nothing but falling snow and shadows.

Everly stepped out of the car. "I'll walk down the road and see if I can get any reception."

"Don't go too far."

"Relax, Mom," Everly said, rolling her eyes.

She zipped her coat up and tugged her beanie snug over her ears, heading off into the darkness.

Jocelin watched her daughter until the light radiating from Everly's phone became a blip in the night reminiscent of a fallen star.

"Be careful!" Jocelin yelled.

Everly yelled something back, but the words were indecipherable over the howling wind. The snowstorm worsened. Jocelin cursed herself for letting Everly go off alone. She was about to chase after her when a pair of headlights lit up the night, traversing the bend they had previously driven around.

She stopped in her tracks, peering at the approaching vehicle.

An old Dodge Ram came into view. Chains were wrapped around the aggressively treaded tires, and a plow clanged on the front end.

The truck pulled up alongside the unremarkable wreck.

Jocelin discerned a bulky frame behind the steering wheel, but any distinguishable features were hidden in the unlit interior of the truck.

The driver-side window lowered.

"Do you require assistance?" asked a man. His voice was so soft it sounded like a whisper.

"Umm," Jocelin hesitated. "I was just calling a tow. . ."

"There's no need for that." The words came out as gentle as the touch of a snowflake. "Excuse me?"

"I'll pull you out myself."

Jocelin was apprehensive to trust the stranger. "No, really it's okay."

He shined a flashlight on her, blinding her.

She held her hands up to shield herself from the abrasive light shining in her eyes. "Hey!" "Can't leave you out here in the middle of a snowstorm."

He climbed out of the truck and stood in front of Jocelin. The flashlight was still fixed on her, but it was easy to gauge the size of the man.

He towered above her, a giant. Narrow-shouldered, yet long-limbed. She imagined his wingspan alone was equal to her height.

She retreated a step.

"Easy," he stated, walking sluggishly toward the back of the truck, where he dropped the tailgate. "I have a chain back here somewhere. I'll strap you up to my trailer hitch and have you out in no time."

Jocelin thought about dismissing him but reconsidered. Here this man was trying to be a good Samaritan, and she was uncomfortable by the kindness. She wondered what that said about the world at large.

"Okay," she said, deciding to accept the offer. "Thank you so much."

The giant located what was presumably the chain and closed the tailgate. Jocelin inched forward to get a better look out of curiosity.

He turned to face her, holding the flashlight downward at his side. In his other hand, he held a tire iron.

"No, I don't have a flat–"

Her explanation was interrupted as the giant struck the top of her head with the procession of a slaughterhouse operator.

Confusion hit her first, then the pain, as she fell into the snow.

The giant scooped her up and tossed her over his shoulder. Blood flowed in a rivulet from the fresh wound, dotting the white snow red. He headed around to the passenger side and opened the door, throwing her inside. Her chin dipped to her chest, slipping out of consciousness and into a sleep as dark as the moonless night.

The truck sank, as the giant got inside the cab.

Unbeknownst to him, Everly had seen the horrific and surreal scene unfold, hiding in the cover of night. She watched as the truck jerked into motion. Panicking, Everly dialed 911 repeatedly, but the calls were instantly dropped due to the lack of service. She ducked as the truck crept by.

"Okay, okay," she said to herself, as her voice hitched.

Acting on impulse, she rose from the shadows and scaled the side of the slow-moving truck, rolling into the bed. The heavy curtain of nightfall helped hide her from being seen in the rearview mirrors. The wind assisted in muffling the noise. And the giant drove onward, unaware of the disturbance in the back of his truck.

Jocelin's eyes fluttered open, and a sharp throbbing sensation greeted her upon waking. Wincing against the pain, she tried to place her whereabouts. Dazed and slumped on the ground, she attempted to stand but was struck with terror when she realized her ankles were bound with nylon rope. As were her hands, which were tied behind her back. Forcing composure, she tilted her head to take in the structure she'd awoken in. It appeared to be a work shed of some variation that was still under construction. The walls were nothing more than plastic films stapled to the wooden frame, and the roof consisted of slabs of plywood. Bundles of insulation were stacked in the corner of the shed. Bits of fiberglass splintered off the bundles from the wind and drifted across the cold cement floor into Jocelin's face. Itchy, she rubbed her forehead against the floor, leaving behind a streak of congealed blood.

She recalled the blow to the head from earlier and the mysterious giant who had delivered it. What happened afterward was unclear, except for a dreamy sequence in which the giant had tossed her into the cab of his truck.

She writhed on the floor, fighting against her restraints. The movement stirred up sawdust and pieces of fiberglass. Her cheek pressed against the floor, she opened her mouth and cried for help. Particles of construction debris rushed to silence her, causing her to cough hard.

A tarp nailed to the door frame curtained the entrance. A square construction light sat on the floor, tilted upwards, illuminating the inside of the shed. The thick power cord ran underneath the tarp and connected to a power source somewhere outside. A door lay flat across a pair of sawhorses, acting as a makeshift workbench. A lumpy mass was perched on top. Jocelin craned her neck for a better look.

It was a dead deer. Steam rose in the freezing air from the corpse. Blood oozed and spilled off the improvised table, pooling on the floor. The creature's jagged antlers cast shadow puppets against the plastic film.

Footsteps stole Jocelin's attention away from the carcass.

Jocelin released a bloodcurdling scream.

"You can do that, it's okay," the giant said, lifting the flap of the tarp aside and ducking his head underneath the doorframe. "Go ahead. Scream."

To her chagrin, she obliged him, screaming for help until her lungs were about to burst. "No one will hear you out here in this place of desolation," he explained softly. "But I understand it's natural, so please. Do what you feel you must."

He approached the workbench, carrying a large toolbox. Studying the carcass, he nodded in solemn approval. He hauled the toolbox on top of the bench next to the dead animal. After unlatching and opening the lid, he began rifling through the toolbox. Tools clanked, the sound reverberating in the near-empty shed. He soon located the specific tool he sought. A folding hand saw.

Ignoring Jocelin's shrieks, he unfurled the sawblade and began to hack off the deer's head.

Jocelin's shrieks dissolved into whimpers, and finally, she pleaded. "Please, let me go."

"Don't do that," he said in a calm tone.

"Pl-please. . ."

He turned to face her, shaking his head. "I permitted your screams, but didn't permit your begging."

"I won't tell anyone," she sobbed. "I won't go to the cops. . ."

Disregarding her proposition, he asked, "Do you wish to know my intent?" "Huh? Wh-what?"

"Consider me an artist," he said, squatting down in front of Jocelin. He held the decapitated deer head by the antlers up for her inspection. Blood from the head dripped onto the floor, merging with her own from the leaking wound on her scalp. "A vision of an abomination

haunts me. . . the image of a deer woman stalks my dreams. My hope is that by sewing this head onto your body, my current obsession will at last come to an end."

Jocelin's eyes bulged, and her mouth widened.

The giant cupped the side of her face in his enormous palm. "Shh, shh," he soothed. She recoiled from his touch.

"Fuck you!" she yelled, her fear morphing into rage. She spat into his face, wishing it were venom.

Using the backside of his hand to wipe away the dribble, the giant snorted in mild irritation. Leisurely, he rolled her over onto her stomach and gripped the rope tied around her wrists. He proceeded to drag her across the floor toward the center of the shed, where a hook hung from a wooden ceiling beam. She contorted her body in protest, but he didn't relent.

Yanked to her feet, her shoulders felt as though they were going to dislocate. The giant hoisted her onto the hook by her shackled wrists. The balls of her feet narrowly touched the floor, allowing for a degree of purchase.

The giant returned to the workbench to retrieve the hand saw.

Jocelin continued to fight, attempting to pry the rope apart. The struggle only tightened her restraints further, the friction burning her skin raw.

Hope faded as reality set in.

Tinges of comfort hit her, knowing her daughter had escaped this pocket of hell. She wished she could rewind time to when they were bickering in the car. Over what, she couldn't even remember now. She longed to hold her daughter like she did back when she was a child. Memories flickered by in rapid succession, and she assumed her life was flashing before her eyes, as death waited to claim her.

All too often are lives cut tragically short by the hands of monsters walking among us. They have no right to wear the cloak of the reaper, yet they have the audacity to borrow it without consent.

Outside, Everly had listened to her mother's wailing. She knew she had to act. Searching the bed of the truck for something to wield as a weapon, her hands landed on an object in the darkness. Clenching it, she slinked over the side of the truck, plunging into the piled snow.

The giant pinched Jocelin's chin between his meaty thumb and index finger, tilting her head side to side, like a butcher examining a hunk of meat. She wriggled on the hook like an impaled worm before being cast into dark waters.

He sighed heavily as if bracing himself for the task at hand.

A chore that needed to be done.

"Okay," he said.

A rush of wind flapped the plastic walls and carried snow flurries into the shed. He palmed her skull and forced her to stare at the floor.

The instinct to survive dwindled.

She visualized her daughter's face and repeated her name in her mind like a prayer.

Everly.

Everly.

Everly.

The teeth of the saw nibbled at her skin, as the blade was pressed against the back of her neck. She closed her eyes in acceptance.

There was a loud and violent *crack* followed by the sound of something heavy hitting the floor.

"Mom!"

Jocelin shot her head up at being called.

Everly stood there, quivering, behind the fallen giant. She held the tire iron in a shaky hand, the tool smeared with blood. She dropped tire iron in favor of the saw, swiping it from the giant's limp hand.

Everly tiptoed around the massive lump on the floor. "Are you okay, Mom!?" "I-I'm okay," she managed.

Everly kneeled and started to cut through the rope bounding her mother's feet together. The giant grumbled.

"Hurry!" Jocelin whispered.

"I'm trying!"

Threads tore.

Jocelin stood and lifted her hands off the hook. She held them out for Everly to start working on the rope tying them together.

The giant stirred in his trauma-induced slumber.

"Everly," Jocelin said in a low voice. "Go."

"Wh-what?"

"Go! Get out of here."

Everly broke into hysterical tears. "No way! I can't leave you, Mom!"

"Just goddamn listen to me!"

"B-but..."

"Run, Ev! Run!"

Everly's face was a runny mess of tears and snot, as she backed away.

"That's my girl," Jocelin said.

Everly turned around and stumbled toward the entrance. She was nearly out of the shed when Jocelin screamed.

Looking over her shoulder, Everly realized she should've run.

The giant stood behind her, teetering. His face was broken. An eyeball hung out of a shattered socket, a cheekbone crushed. Chipped teeth protruded through his lips. What was once a nose was an unrecognizable bulge of bony mush.

Everly stuttered, tongue-tied by fear.

The giant lurched at her but stopped abruptly. Frozen in place like a snapshot from a forgotten Polaroid. A look of disbelief was painted across his face.

He collapsed.

Jocelin stood over the giant.

Grasped between her tethered hands was the tire iron.

Jocelin swung again and again, bashing the giant's head. She panted, as blood fissured from his cracked skull. Red flowed across the sawdust floor.

She didn't stop until Everly called her.

"Mom…"

Jocelin slowly let go of the tire iron.

Everly rushed to embrace her mother.

All the trivial arguments evaporated.

The blizzard raged, infiltrating the shed, and enveloping the pair in wintry swirls. They held each other tighter than they had in years.

Together, warm and safe against the cold world.

We Aren't Salem Here

by Isabelle Palerma

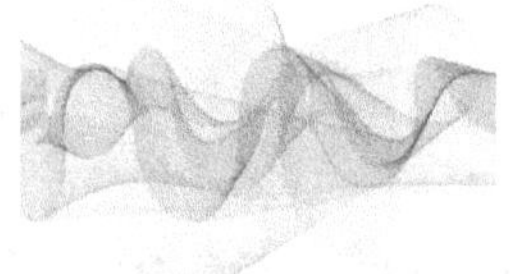

As time unspooled from the center, the twins' appearances metamorphosed. Dahlia's hair looked as though it was crafted of dandelion wisps, bleached white as bone. Her piercing gaze was direct, although her responses were evasive.

Ophelia had a cloud of rust-colored hair. She harbored secrets in her chest like ships coming to shore inside of her rib cage. She couldn't look villagers in the eye. Though something about her appearance intimidated many, Jonathan Nelson was beguiled by her.

On rare nights, villagers saw their sister Bethany sitting outside of the lighthouse, violin tucked underneath her chin, playing concertos to the sea-storms. She, too, had a faraway look in her eyes.

They emerged from the lighthouse they called home occasionally. When the fog was heavy and the shoals of bream retreated, they sat in the gray sands, a faded blanket beneath them. Their faces were dusty and drawn. They wore ashen, earth-tone dresses - Ophelia in the color of natural clay and Dahlia in the color of a wet stone.

Around midnight, the girls picnicked at the edge of the forest. They approached the clove currant shrubs and collected the fragrant, black fruits in the skirts of their dresses. Dahlia and Ophelia had secrets, but their whispers were scritch-scratches that made the townsfolk uncomfortable.

Some suspected Bethany was their caretaker. They had claimed to see her yellow-brown Volkswagen Beetle on the ferry. Others spoke of seeing her working a secretarial job, sitting at a mint-green typewriter.

The twins appeared fragile like porcelain dolls, limbs sharp angles and awkward, yet their jade eyes haunting. Something about the dullness of their gazes disquieted people.

An old man, Jasper Renfroe, had told Madge Belcher that he had heard the twins speaking in a made-up language. He hadn't understood what the two said, but he knew it was unlike any language he had ever heard. Madge, the gossip, had spread the story.

One gloomy Thursday evening, they rode into town on a powder blue tandem bicycle. Gray clouds had burst, and rain began to pummel the buildings. From underneath the awning of the drugstore, they watched as villagers darted out of the rain.

Their arms linked in one another's, their steps synchronized, the girls entered the shop. Neither Dahlia nor Ophelia noticed the shoppers' stares as they meandered to the soda fountain counter. They murmured in their own language and shared a vanilla egg cream.

Did they not know the rumors spoken about them?

Jonathan paused at a display of bandages and glanced at the soda fountain's chrome and vinyl stools. Seeing Ophelia's cloud of hair piled in a topknot from behind, he approached them.

He inhaled deeply before tapping Ophelia on the shoulder. She looked back, her eyes wide and startled. Her scent engulfed him: the smell of bonfires and cinnamon sticks. A moment later, broken out of the spell, he remembered why he had approached them.

He leaned his mouth toward her alabaster ear and spoke into it. Dahlia watched, taking a spoonful of egg cream fizz into her mouth.

The rustle of his voice in her ear bewildered Ophelia, yet he enchanted her. The way his eyes sparkled - the silver-blue irises with golden rings around his pupil. His scent - like orange peels and pine needles. His voice - husky and rich. She remained silent as he spoke. After he walked away, Ophelia dared to speak. Swiveling her stool to face Dahlia, a grave expression on her face, she took a sip of the syrupy drink.

Neither spoke, yet concern gleamed in both pairs of eyes. Ophelia finally revealed what Jonathan had said to her. She murmured to her sister in their made-up language, "He said we need to be careful."

"Careful of what?" Dahlia replied as she twisted her fingers around one another in a fidgety game of sorts, not lifting her gaze.

"I'm not sure exactly," Ophelia admitted and dropped her voice, a solemn expression on her face. "He did say some of the townsfolk are wary of us."

"Wary?" Dahlia echoed.

Dahlia took a long sip from her straw, then glanced up at her sister. "What have we given them to be wary of?"

Ophelia rubbed her temples and gnawed on her lower lip. "I don't know."

The two fell silent, aside from the occasional slurps of the drink.

They left without speaking, slipping a single bill onto the countertop. The rain roared, furious, as the wind battered metal street signs and howled. All night, the twins huddled into one another, whispering to determine what it was about them that made the villagers so uncomfortable.

When Bethany got home, she watched them shiver and asked them if they had eaten. Dahlia smoothed her dress and looked up at her older sister with a mournful stare. Bethany's mouth was set in a thin line as she bustled around the kitchen. Pots and pans rattled as she placed a cast-iron pan in the oven. She pulled the yellow cornmeal off a shelf and shook her head as she mixed the dry ingredients.

As the skillet heated, Bethany asked Ophelia and Dahlia about their day. "We went into town," Dahlia told her as Ophelia played with their pet rabbit. Bethany nodded, whisking the liquids, then yanked the pan out of the oven and coated it with butter.

"What was there to do in town?" Bethany asked her sisters, waiting for the cornbread to cook.

"Not much," Ophelia admitted. "We went to the drugstore."

"Get anything? Do they still sell those wooden puzzles you both like?"

Dahlia and Ophelia looked at her, their eyes wide open with surprise. "We didn't look," they told her in unison as she slipped out of her work dress and into her soft cotton pajamas. "We got an egg cream. A vanilla one," Dahlia told Bethany, a smile on her face. "Jonathan Nelson talked to Ophelia."

Bethany grinned as she got a glass jug of milk out of the refrigerator. "Oh?"

Dahlia, Ophelia, and Bethany had gone to church when they were young, and their parents were alive. The girls had seen the Nelsons at services. Vera Nelson was a stern-looking woman yet always wore frivolous hats. Dahlia and Ophelia had stared at the middle child, Jonathan Nelson.

His silver-blue eyes had shimmered whenever he looked in the girls' direction.

"Think he might be in love with Ophelia." Dahlia hid her smile behind her hand, self-conscious of her crooked teeth. Ophelia turned a light pink shade as she took the utensils out of the drawer.

"He's not in love with me," Ophelia insisted. "He was warning us," she mumbled.

Bethany's smile vanished. "Warning you?" she echoed. "What would he be warning you about?"

Ophelia took a deep breath. "It's the other townsfolk," she told Bethany. "They don't trust us."

"How so? Isn't the heart of every man wicked?" Bethany responded, her hand trembling at the knob on the stovetop.

All three fell silent. Bethany tore apart the hot cornbread and gave each a hunk with butter. They chewed without speaking. That night, instead of playing her violin outside with the winds churning around her, Bethany ascended to her room, locked the door behind her, and played sorrowful songs.

As Ophelia and Dahlia washed the dishes and put them away, Bethany stuck her head out her bedroom door and called down to them, "Stay inside tonight, girls, you hear?"

"But the mists are calling," Dahlia called back.

"Stay inside." Her voice had taken on a reproachful tone.

And so, they did.

The twins sat on their beds, Ophelia petting their rabbit and Dahlia knitting. Bethany had stopped playing the violin. The rain bashed against the stone, and the three fell asleep to the sounds of the storm.

The girls had picked clove currants earlier that week, and after Bethany made them each a bowl of oatmeal, they deposited the fruits into the gloppy, beige mix. The currants added a flavor they liked very much, yet Ophelia turned to Dahlia. Speaking in their own language, Ophelia said under her breath, "It tastes awful, doesn't it?"

Dahlia, not seeking to offend her sister, did not reply, but when Bethany's back was turned, she nodded in agreement.

Bethany paced the galley kitchen, her steps short. "We need to figure out what the townsfolk are saying," she mumbled.

The twins raised their stony eyes to their sister, gazing at her. As they stared at her, Bethany regarded them with the dispassionate regard of a stranger, wondering what it was that the townsfolk were saying.

Bethany shook her head and commanded Ophelia to get her boar hairbrush from the bathroom, so she could brush the girls' frizzy hair into submission. Something about the stiffness of the bristles smoothing their hair subdued them. The three walked up the stairs into the twins' bedroom and sat on Dahlia's bed.

The bed frame groaned at the weight of the three sisters, though, truth be told, all three were light. After their baths, when drying off, one could see every notch of bone in their spines. Yet, the bed was an antique, and thus, complained when the girls climbed on top of it.

Bethany told the girls old fairy tales from Germany, the ones with the dark endings: women impregnated in their sleep, or the story of a maiden forced to dance wearing scorching-hot shoes made of iron until she died or a prince falling into thorny brambles and blinding himself. They listened, rapt, their attention unwavering.

Dahlia clutched their rabbit as though he were a lovey and not a live rabbit. As the sky grayed and the rain fell, they sat on the bed and talked, telling one another stories of make-believe and memories of once upon a time when their parents were alive.

That evening, after they finished their watery stew, the twins turned to Bethany, their typically dead-eyed gazes pleading.

She fussed with the dishes in the sink, then looked first at Dahlia, then Ophelia. "What?" she demanded.

"There's a festival in town," Dahlia said with a giggle, covering her mouth.

"A festival of fishes," Ophelia added. "They'll be decorating people like mermaids. Men are dressing as pirates, and they are auctioning off treasures of the sea."

"And selling necklaces made of cockles."

Bethany arched an eyebrow. "And I suppose you two would like to go?"

They nodded, offering Bethany their best pouts.

Bethany glanced out a small round window and saw the gray clouds approaching from the sea.

"I suppose you can go," she answered with a reluctant smile. "But..." she added, "I want you to go upstairs and find your rain boots. It looks like a nor'easter might be blowing through."

The twins scurried up the cramped, winding staircase to their bedroom and peeled their nightgowns off, slipping into simple dresses. They grumbled to one another about Bethany's demand for them to wear galoshes but pulled the rubber boots on regardless.

"Will we take the Volkswagen?" Ophelia asked Bethany once downstairs as Dahlia was saying, "Can we buy necklaces?"

Without waiting for a response, Ophelia added, "Can we watch the play?"

They crossed the wet sand.

"You know," Bethany chided, "for two young women who stay to themselves most of the day, you seem to know an awful lot about this festival of fishes."

Dahlia leaned and whispered a secret in Bethany's ear.

"What did you tell her?" Ophelia demanded as they squelched in the muddy grass, crossing the field to Bethany's car.

"I told her that the reason you want to see the play is because Jonathan is in it."

"That is not true." Ophelia crossed her arms over her chest. "At the performance, they will be announcing a Coral Queen, and I want to see who they crown."

Bethany stared at the road as the rain came down harder. Thunder roared. She could scarcely see the stripes on the pavement as she drove. Lightning shattered the porcelain cornflower sky. None of the sisters spoke.

Once they arrived in the town square, the scene was like a tableau. Patrons with cash in hand. Sellers displaying necklaces of seashells and flaunting treasures from the sea. Their gazes shifted from one another to the sisters.

Rain drenched the tent canopies. The showers soaked the villagers. Yet still, they stared. A distant wind whistled. Silence persisted. Bethany drew her sisters near. The briny smell of the ocean wafted over the people.

Jonathan strode toward the three sisters, undeterred by scowls and glares. His mother reached out to grab him, her frivolous church hat askew. The rain continued to fall from the sky. When near, he spoke in a low voice and said, "We may not be Salem, but people around here have their prejudices. I warned you to be careful."

"We have been careful," Dahlia responded, a guarded expression on her face.

Bethany did not speak but took a couple of steps backward, her footsteps clattering on the cobblestone.

"Everyone makes sacrifices," Jonathan told them, his tone ominous.

"What are you saying, Jonathan?" Ophelia murmured.

"I. . . All I'm trying to say is—"

Jasper stepped forward, his brown, beady eyes glittering with rage. Thunder cracked. He rasped, "The boy does not know what he's saying. He's an idiot."

Vera Nelson cried out, aghast at the suggestion.

"You are not welcome here," Madge hissed, her gaze cutting through them like shears through cloth.

The twins glanced at one another as a gigantic bolt of lightning flashed across the sky. They linked arms, clutching one another so tightly their knuckles whitened. Neither noticed Bethany scrambling away from them and scurrying back to her car.

The small courtyard became claustrophobic with the cluster of townsfolk surrounding the twins. A knot of people circled them. Something about it all made Dahlia and Ophelia uneasy. That was before the first accusation.

The villagers levied a variety of complaints against the girls, culminating in blaming them for the ceaseless rainstorms the island had been experiencing that summer. Once accused, the twins fell silent as though stones weighed down their tongues.

Jonathan stood near them, looking small and frightened. "Everyone makes sacrifices," he muttered again.

Ophelia untangled herself from her twin. She reached out and grasped his hands. "What more sacrifices must we make? We already lost our parents. We live on the outskirts of the shores. It is just us and our sister. All we have is one another," she told Jonathan, her eyes glistening with tears.

"Not for much longer," Jasper wheezed as he approached them.

Dahlia twisted her fingers through her coarse blonde hair, mouth agape. "Wh-what does he mean by that?"

The mob tightened the circle around them.

Jasper fumbled around and produced a length of jute. With a surprising amount of force, he shoved Jonathan away from the girls.

A mess of hands yanked and tugged at the rope, creating and tightening knots at each girl's wrists. Some villagers spat on the girls. Others shrieked curses at them. People pushed Ophelia and Dahlia. Some grabbed their hair and pulled clumps of it out. Tears streamed down the girls' cheeks.

"I tried warning you," Jonathan whispered, "We aren't Salem here, but people around here have their prejudices."

His whispers were lost to the shouts of the townsfolk.

The ropes burned at Dahlia and Ophelia's wrists. The rain continued to pour. Lightning struck and thunder roared. Early evening was waning. The night began to fall.

"You are responsible for these storms," Madge sneered. "It wasn't until you lot came 'round that we experienced dark, stormy nights like these. You are witches. You brought the storms with you. We used to have sunshine. People used to ruddy their skin with sunlight. For months, all we've known is storms. Nor'easters and hurricanes."

The girls dropped their gazes, and both began to speak in unison, but no one understood.

"It's voodoo," exclaimed Jonathan's mother.

The twins glanced up. Dahlia looked at the woman plaintively. "But, Mrs. Nelson," she whispered, "we know you from church services."

Vera Nelson shook her head. "I haven't seen either of you at a service in years. You might as well be heathens."

Jonathan shot his mother a pleading glance. "Ma," he exclaimed, "You know Ophelia and Dahlia. This is wrong. We aren't Salem. We're not like those folks and their trials."

His mother looked away. "I don't know these girls. Not any more than they know you."

A hush fell. Sickly gray-green clouds swirled above them. The air sizzled electric before another bolt of lightning shattered across the dome of the sky. Jasper and Madge each grabbed one of the girls by the arm, hooking a scrawny arm underneath an armpit, and dragged them out of the town square.

"Please," Ophelia sobbed, "Where are you taking us?"

"You can't do this," Dahlia insisted, "We haven't done anything wrong."

The townsfolk trailed behind. Clouds billowed overhead. Rain poured. Thunder boomed, shaking the earth. The girls' skin blanched from loss of blood flow. They no longer spoke.

No longer cried.

No longer moved.

When they regained consciousness, it was dawn. The girls' empty eyes rolled around like frosted jade marbles empty in a dead skull. Neither spoke. Their mouths were dry. Their teeth felt as though they were rotting. Madge hoisted Ophelia up on a tree limb, wrapping rope around her thin, perfect throat. Jasper suspended Dahlia from a different branch, a similar noose around her neck.

"Maybe now, the storms will stop."

"People 'round here have their prejudices," Jonathan whispered, sinking against the tree trunk.

He swore he heard them whisper, but later, he told the others it was the rustling of leaves.

When the town awoke and ascended the hill to see the twins, their corpses swung.

Everyone makes sacrifices.

"Maybe now, the storms will stop," Madge had whispered. Though the skies were gray, a silver sun had risen. A few birds chirped. A new day dawned.

It was only after the bodies had been cut down a few hours later that the storms began again.

Moms

by Scott Russell Duncan

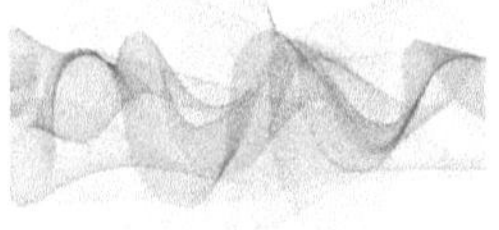

Out of boredom, you drag out the box with the big blue button. The one your mom gave you, not that you remember her. When you were a kid, you asked your dad about the button and he snorted, "It was your Mom's." At least you think he said that.

"What does it do?" you asked.

"I've got no idea," Dad said, radiated by the TV glow. "Figure it out on your own." You never did, not really.

Now you're older. Old enough to tolerate some mystery, but not the one you've kept on your dresser all this time. Big as an old cell phone, the case is concrete white and porous like lava rock. And the button itself is broken. At least the last time you pressed it, nothing happened. You sit on the bed and cradle the box and slowly press the blue circle down. Nothing. You machinegun mash the button. Nothing. The box slips to your lap. Your finger throbs. *Maybe I'm pressing the wrong button.*

You flip the box over and set it on the floor, making the box the button and the button the box. You gently step down on the inverse button with your foot. There is a single click, and then something whirls inside, and it sounds like a city generator flipping on. The box grows, becomes monolithic, and swallows you. The world rumbles like a vacuum cleaner. Space is tight yet the hours that pass lull you to sleep and when you wake you're sure something awful has happened, that your button pressing has destroyed the universe. Maybe you are all that is left of mankind. You hope this and sleep but then the rumbling ceases and the monolith sighs.

It's still. The top disintegrates. You see that you are on a shore by a black mud pit ocean. All around you is a ring of phosphorescent rocks— monoliths, like yours. The sea is dark, and it smells like motor oil.

A mob of heads, a rainbow of monster heads, peers down on you. Their rows of eyes blink, and they clasp their flippers together. You think you know them.

"Here he is!" a green one says.

"He is big," an orange one says.

Chorus— "Oh yes, much bigger than before."

The green one reaches in with giant flippers and pulls you out easily as if you were filled with bubble wrap and moss, not organs and bone.

"Who are you?" you whine, ready to be eaten.

The monster, twenty feet tall, body like a land shark and a head like an air balloon, holds you up in front of its dark green face covered in a hideous crowd of eyes.

"I'm your mother," it smiles, all eyes glittering.

Your father never really talked about Mom except to say that she was a freak, and you were lucky to be away from her. For all you know, this weirdo could be your Mom. Your costumed steroid cultist Mom.

Different colored heads of the other creatures stand close, hordes of eyes on you.

"Well, who are they?"

Chorus—"We're your mothers too!"

The green one sets you down on a glowing stone couch.

The Moms-monsters crowd you and give you wet green-yellow-orange-blue kisses. You cringe.

In the center of the thin-lipped kiss whirlwind, the tingly acidic saliva, the fish-cold flesh, and glances into the many sets of eyes all filled with maternity, prove to you that your Moms aren't human. And that they love you.

Blue Mom says, "Now tell us what you have been up to since you were born."

You wipe your face on your sleeve. Mom spit burns holes in it, but not you. "Well, you mean I'm not human?" you say.

"Not all the way . . . not from our side certainly."

All Moms look at the Red Mom, who says, "None from me either!"

"Oh," you say, and an ancient knot inside you loosens.

"That explains everything, so I'm an alien."

"No," Purple Mom tells you. "Your father is from Earth, sweetheart."

"All of you are my mother?"

Chorus—"Only mothers you will ever have."

"So, Dad . . . Dad had . . . intercourse with all of you."

Yellow Mom pets your head. "That's the way it works, little one."

Purple Mom cries, jets of water streaming up her collection of eyes, and falling, splashing on you.

"I'm so glad we had this little talk with him," Purple Mom says.

Your Moms console each other: "He is so big." "So advanced for his age and so precious." "Enjoy him now; he'll be grown in no time."

"I am grown, Moms," you interrupt.

Chorus— "Of course you are dear."

"Did you Moms send me to spy on the Earth? Because if you want me to blow it up or anything, I will. I hate the Earth."

Moms look at each other.

For a second you think they are going to eat you after all. Then, they all converge on you in a giant crushing mom-hug.

Chorus— "You are our special boy!"

Red Mom settles next to you and holds your hand between her flippers.

"Now, sweetheart, tell us mommies what you have been doing since you were born. Seeing as you never call."

Maybe this is what you stayed on Earth for. Maybe this has been your purpose, to tell the universe (well, your Moms) what the Earth has put you through. The human condition. You start from the beginning and after a while, you wonder if it all was really like the way you tell it, it seems surreal and full of bullshit, but you can't remember any other way. You tell your Moms of the burden of life, the many stinks, the humiliation, and the bestial hierarchy of human society. You tell them how the other kids would steal your shoes. And about having to remember so many things so living won't be harder, brushing your teeth, keeping your house key safe, getting the generic brand and jumbo size because it's economical. You rant on about the teeter-totter of loneliness and misanthropy, but as you speak, you see Moms's unblinking faces nod and mutter umm's, oh's, and uh-huh's. And you wonder if they truly heard you.

At the end of your life story, you sob out, "So that's it, mommies."

Chorus— "That was a great story sweetie." Red-Blue-Yellow hug.

Chorus— "We are so proud of our little boy."

Green Mom tries to tickle your stomach but the skin on her flipper is abrasive. "It makes us sad, but it's time for our little sweetie to go home."

You look up from hugging Yellow and Red Moms.

"No Mom, I want to stay here, with you guys, I mean you, Moms."

"If only you could sweetheart," Yellow Mom coos at you.

"Before we forget, we have a birthday present for you."

In your hands, slathered with mom-mucus, your mothers slide a small spacesuit big enough for a toddler or a monkey. Some Mom smoothed down your hair and stuck a party hat on your head.

"Thanks, moms, but I'm grown now. I'm too big for this."

Chorus— "Really?"

Flippers pull back your head and force their way into your mouth.

"I guess you are," Red Mom says. She feels where your wisdom teeth used to be, making you feel sleepy.

"Oh, that's different," Green Mom says, "We held something for you for when you were big enough. A family heirloom."

From under the glowing stone couch, Green Mom pulls out a box, concrete-white and porous. A box with a big black button.

"Hope it fits sweetheart. It was your grandpa's before he died."

"Oh," you say. "Another button."

Red Mom frowns, "Don't be ungrateful, a lot of boys would like a button."

"What does it do?"

Moms look at each other.

Chorus— "You press it."

"He really takes after his father," Yellow Mom sighs.

They pull you up by your arms.

Chorus— "Better leave now our little man. Back to that big bad planet."

You go limp and slide through flippers. You run and clutch an indigo-colored mother who moos whale static.

"I don't want to go back, I don't fit in there," you cry. "I love you, Moms."

The Green Mom gently pulls you off.

"That one isn't your mother—Sorry, he is rambunctious. Yes, a mixed coupling."

They drag you to the monolith and put you in. You clutch the box with a black button and the too-small-spacesuit.

"Moms! Don't leave me, Moms," you squeal in the high-pitched tongue of your people, your Moms.

Chorus— "Bye-bye sweetie. Take care."

The top shuts. The world shudders. Earth will have to do.

The Witches Ball

by Elaine Marie Carnegie-Padgett

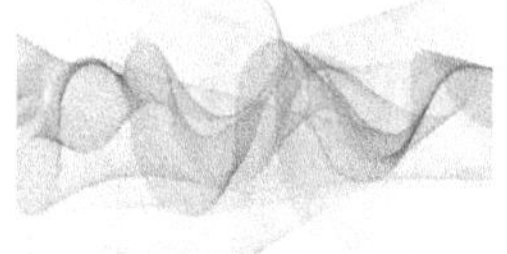

Ten-year-old Meredith bounced in through the door and slammed it behind her, plopped onto the divan with her arms crossed firmly over her chest. "Ma will *not* let me attend the Witches Ball, *again*. It is a holiday! Our *greatest* celebration, the festival of Samhain is the hallowed evening when we dress in costume and gather to give thanks while the mortal children go door to door, trick-or-treating. Ma won't let me do anything. Nothing at all! Not even trick-or-treating with my friends."

"Your Ma has her reasons, I'm sure," Agatha said, although she knew full well why her sister would not allow Meredith out tonight.

"She said I can't go until I am older," Meredith scoffed. "I am planning to ask for redress. Perhaps a year away from the Coven and her magic will allow her to remember she has a daughter!"

"You don't mean it, Meredith. You can't ask for redress because you are mad at your Ma. She has her reasons."

"If she does not relent, or at least explain . . .
I *will* make my redress tonight on All Hallows Eve
at the gathering of the Covens . . . *at the Witches
Ball* . . . even though she has forbidden it."

Agatha levitated a cup of warm chocolate to
Meredith with just a wee scant of magic to calm
her nerves.

"Thank you, Auntie." Meredith took a sip.
"Ma probably doesn't even remember I like warm
chocolate." She sat back feeling sorry for herself. "I
don't understand what happened. We used to be
so close and now she has entirely shut me out. I'm
sure it would be different if my Da were here."

"Have you asked her about it?"

"I have. She told me I was talking nonsense.
Let's go for a ride, Auntie." Meredith smiled at
Agatha. "Ma won't mind if I am with you. She
snapped her fingers, and they were at the family
tree. "Let's go," she called and zoomed out of sight.

Agatha joined her, surprised. *She is quite
accomplished. She's been riding when her mother
strictly forbade it. I wonder what else Meredith has
been up to.* Agatha watched her laughing and
shouting and racing with her friends above the
clouds. *Yes . . . it is as I feared. At Meredith's age,
we were into all kinds of magic mischief . . . but we
did not have a curse looming over us.*

"I am chilled to the bone, dear Meredith. Let's pop home for some warmed chocolate and cookies."

Meredith grinned at her and snapped her fingers. Agatha found herself in the Coven House watching while Meredith conjured a blazing fire.

Agatha went to the kitchen to gather herself and put together chocolate and cookies. The pair lounged on the rugs before the fireplace to ward off the cold.

"It is difficult not to be surprised, Meredith. Did you show me your prowess today in defiance of your mother for a reason?"

"No, I am tired of hiding and skulking. I have a friend who advised me to speak to her first. I won't pretend anymore, and she won't notice anyway, Aunt Aggie. She's never here."

"Notice what?" Adelheid said in a shocked voice.

"Me. . ." Meredith scoffed at her mother.

"I don't understand why you are so angry all the time."

"You won't tell me what's wrong. I know *something* is wrong, Ma. Maybe, if you were home more often. . ." Meredith levitated the snacks to the kitchen. She stood and snapped her fingers, dressed for riding, she announced, "I'm going out."

Adelheid stood, mouth gaping, and stared at her daughter. "You are not going anywhere, young lady, except to your room!" she said, waved her hand, and Meredith disappeared.

Adelheid looked at Agatha. "What is going on?"

"That won't hold her. Meredith has been honing her magic and hiding her skill. It is time for you to tell her the truth, at least you will be close to her if she needs you."

"Absolutely not!" Adelheid said. "I might put her in danger too. I can't."

"Better the devil you know. . ." Agatha insisted and left her to it. Agatha found peace in the forest. She walked in the shaded canopy of the far-off wood listening to the voices of the trees.

"Agatha," Adelheid cried, jolting her from the peaceful meandering. "Agatha, come quickly."

Adelheid was in a furor, pacing back and forth. "She's gone."

"Did you call her?"

"Of course, I called. I tried to go to her with no result and then I scried for her. It's All Hallows Eve. She is especially vulnerable tonight."

"She's worked up a personal protection spell," Agatha chuckled.

"When did she learn that?" Adelheid shouted in frustration. "You know what I have to do. There is the greatest chance I will find him this year as they turn ten."

"What good will it do to find one and lose the other?" Agatha said. "Why won't you share with her? Tell her she has a brother who is missing and let her help."

"I can't do that. She is in danger too." Adelheid sneered at her. "I'm calling the Seven."

"Do what you must, but this may not end well."

Meredith landed in the far-off wood near the Coven Circle and the ancient ritual stones. "Chevrón are you here? Chevrón!" she shouted as he appeared before her.

"What's going on? What happened?"

"It's my mother. We've had a row. If we don't go back now . . . we won't be able to. I can't hide from her forever."

Chevrón sat on the nearest stone. "You must be certain you are not doing this for personal gain."

"What? You getting cold feet?"

"No. You know better than that. It's difficult for a witch to go backward in time and come home. We're more powerful when we're together . . . especially for children. But that is *why* I ask. Are you certain this trip is *not* for personal gain? That would make it harder for us to come home again."

"Something is wrong with Ma. If I find out what it is, then maybe I can help. Maybe it can be like it used to be," Meredith explained as tears welled in her eyes.

"Well, let's get to it then," Chevrón said.

They stood at the ritual stone, shoulder to shoulder. Chevrón nicked his thumb and let his blood drop upon the stone.

"Now me," Meredith nicked her thumb and squeezed until her blood dropped on top of his.

He grasped Meredith's hand and whispered, All *Hallows Eve*, this most powerful night. *All Hallows Eve* join the power of *Samhain*," he whispered and bowed his head. Then they chanted. *"Blood of blood . . . Bone of bone. . ."*

"Look," Chevrón turned his wrist, and a crescent moon with three stars shone, the bright yellow light tumbling within as if it were burning inside the flesh.

"Mine too," Meredith showed her wrist.

"I . . . don't think this is supposed. . ." Chevron began.

The children disappeared and found themselves in the center of the Coven House surrounded by the Seven. The Seven High Priestesses of the Seven Covens. The children were silent knowing this was a powerful and solemn occasion when the Seven Covens gathered.

Adelheid stared at Chevrón. "Who are *you*?" her voice quivered.

He was trembling. "M-Meredith and I are friends."

"Leave him be, Ma," Meredith cried.

Adelheid ignored her and circled the children inside the Circle of Seven.

"Of my blood and of my sight. . . Show me now . . . my children's light."

The Coven began to chant and circle the children. "Ouch. Meredith. It's happening again." Chevrón turned his wrist and the crescent moon, and three stars glowed brightly, but this time the tumbling, burning light was blue. Meredith turned her wrist, identical to his. Hers also shone blue.

Adelheid pulled her collar aside and a smaller version of that same mark burned there on her shoulder. "It is the mark of our family. Your father and I devised it, and you were both born under it. What is your name?" Adelheid whispered.

"Chevrón."

She wept, "You are my son. We have called my child, and two have come. My son, Chevrón, was born and stolen from my arms by magic's curse." She was overcome.

"I'm so sorry, Ma. I didn't know," Meredith cried and held onto her mother.

"When you came of age, I was obsessed," Adelheid spoke to Chevron while comforting her daughter. "I looked for you everywhere. I knew I would find you when your magic matured. . ."

"No!" Chevrón interrupted Adelheid. "My mother died when I was three. You can ask the Maiden Doula at the group home." His voice was high-pitched.

"It is a lie," Adelheid spat. "The Doula attending your birth took you from my arms," she whispered. "The Doula are nurses. Some light and some dark, and they are many."

"No, it's not true. No." Chevrón shook his head and looked at Meredith in a panic.

"It must be so, Chevrón. Look at our wrists. We were both drawn to Mother's call. You are my brother *and* my best friend."

"No." He grabbed Meredith's hand, and they disappeared.

"Call them back," Adelheid shouted. "They don't know the danger. Call them back."

The Seven called and called in vain. They couldn't trace the children.

"It is the curse," Adelheid said. "This is the night."

She was a High Priestess, as was Agatha. Seven High Priestesses of Seven Covens called. The Wizards and Warlocks and Witches of all ilks gathered against the curse. Each with their own children to protect.

Adelaide declared. "This is a summons to battle the curse with the power of the gathered Covens. We will meet at the Circle, near the ritual stones." When all were present, they departed for the far-off wood. They arrived in time to see the children's trace. The Coven Doula lit the sacred fire, and the Covens gathered their magic to call the children back and battle the curse of darkness.

"Look, it's Ma," Meredith whispered. The Doula looked around and Chevrón put a finger to his lips. They watched as Chevrón was born and the Doula took him from his mother, said

"This is the curse of the witching line . . . Now, your son will believe he's mine.

Later I'll take your daughter too, and there's nothing at all . . . that you can do." She laughed wildly.

Chevrón knew it was true. "Stop," he shouted, and the Doula looked at them and a cruel smile played about her lips. She opened her mouth in a grotesque façade. All cavernous mouth with razor-sharpened teeth, black gums, and tongue flapping wildly as she laughed. Her darkness spewed from that chasm and surrounded the children through time. In the time before, the Doula disappeared to Adelheid's screams.

The children watched spellbound by the darkness as Agatha and the warlock ran into the birthing room. They saw Agatha help deliver Meredith while the warlock comforted Adelheid for a witch is powerless while giving birth. They heard him promise to find their son.

"He is our father?" Chevrón asked.

"He never returned," Meredith whispered. "I can't move," she spoke slowly.

Chevrón squirmed and reached for her. He saw her head loll and sway back and forth and shook her.

"Stop it," she shouted at him. "Where are we?"

"Don't forget," he said, his voice soft in the gathering gloom.

She stared straight ahead, her body levitated, "Don't forget," she whispered. Chevrón fought the darkness, but he too succumbed and the children floated concealed in the Doula's darkness. Their mother called. They heard the chanting but could not answer. They watched silently, horrified as particles of their bodies were consumed by the darkness.

"No. Fight it, Meredith. You have to fight!" Chevrón cried. He struggled to kick his legs and reached for his sister's hand. She stared at him, and he could see her spirit, her consciousness fighting to survive. Together they fell to the floor, challenging the Doula's magic.

"Don't let it take you Meredith . . . fight it with your mind and your magic." Chevrón waved his hand in a protective spell around them. It sparkled momentarily and fell in ash as the Doula increased her attack.

"Together," Chevrón whispered. "We are stronger together." They lifted their hands, and the protection sparkled around them, and the gloom receded. It was easier to breathe but they did not lose concentration for each felt the power of the Doula increasing.

The warlock, Declan, trapped in the curse since he found the Doula ten years ago, stirred from the stupor he inflicted upon himself. The curse bound his magic and to save his essence, he lay dormant in a static state. She could not sense him, but neither could he escape her. He felt the strength of her darkness weakening. Declan was transported to the Coven Circle near the ancient ritual stones in the far-off forest intending to enlist the aid of the Covens and found them already there.

"Declan?" Adelheid whispered then shouted and ran to him. He was thin and considerably weakened, but there was no mistaking it was he.

"We must call the Doula to the Coven Circle among our gathered power," he said. "She is many bound by black magic, ancient and strong, I could not overcome it alone. We must invoke the strength of the Ancients to ban and forever disperse her magic. If we are not successful, she will continue to take our children."

The Covens took their places quickly around the wide circle and the High Priestess' spoke the spell.

"In the gathered strength of the ancient runes, the Covens call beneath the moon. In the Mother's bosom, the children rest, the Doula has cursed that which is blessed. We call her now by this ancient rite to answer for this harm tonight."

The covens chanted together, and a brilliant light rose around them as the ancients attended and lent their power. The Doula appeared, and with her in the circle were Meredith and Chevrón who ran to their mother. In the circle appeared a spirit. None recognized her surrounded by the brilliant light.

An eerie voice lent itself to the Circle *"Doula, you have chosen a path of anger and hate and brought yourself unto this fate. None are to blame, no curse remains, disperse dark magic from whence it came."*

The Doula shattered into a million tiny particles in a cloud that exploded through the trees.

The spirit left and the light receded as the Covens gathered round Declan, happy for his return. While the adults rejoiced, Chevrón stole away, and Meredith followed.

"Where are you going?"

"I don't know what to do, Meredith. I have never been someone's *son* . . . or brother."

"Without your courage, the curse could not have been broken. You were brave. You saved me, Chevrón–"

"No. I was terrified," he interrupted his sister.

"What will I do now? I don't know where I–"

"You *are* our son, as you have always been," his father interrupted him.

"I am afraid," Chevron wept, and Meredith held him, weeping too.

"You will come home," Declan whispered, kneeling next to his children and taking them into his arms.

"Are you ready?" Adelheid asked while she stroked her weeping children.

He looked up at his parents and then at his sister, taking his time to really see them and touch the spirit of their love for him. "Yes," he whispered, and Declan took them home.

Encuentros con la Llorona

by Carmen Baca

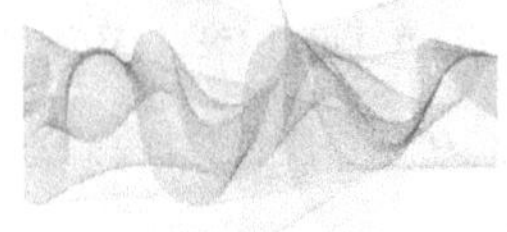

Sprawled on her back after somersaulting onto the grassy riverbank, Bella lay still. No way she was here, her mind reasoned. *But I AM here*, her awareness confirmed. The cool grass beneath her, the fresh breeze blowing the scent of the river over her, the tree boughs soughing in the distance—They proved she was in a verdant meadow somewhere. One minute she had been looking at a photograph of a country scene and the next she had plunged right into it. Sitting up to look around, fourteen-year-old Bella wasn't sure whether to be alarmed, whether she had gone *loca*, or whether she should give herself a good, hard slap to see what good it might do. "What the—," she muttered, rising and then turning in a circle, her eyes darting from the meadow to the forest beyond.

Bella and her parents had been at the family ranch since her father started his two-week summer vacation. Three days into their stay, she had run out of reading material. The ladder standing against the wall of her grandmother's old adobe house enticed her to search the attic, which her parents had been clearing out.

She climbed up and in, standing for a moment to let her eyes adjust. An old, dusty trunk stood against the far-right wall. If there were any books up here, they'd be in there. The next thing she knew after finding the small pile of photograph albums at the bottom and looking down into the first picture, she was tumbling through nothing. Her focus on the photograph had acted as a catalyst by which the world of the forgotten reached out collective arms of welcome and drew her in.

The instinctive fear rising up her spine dissipated like someone had pulled it physically from her body and replaced it with a sense of security. The susto, the shock, which the unknown and surreal produced, instead turned to curiosity. *Where was she? Why was she here? What*—the questions multiplied. She needed answers. Then she needed to get away.

"Hello," she called. The meadow was surrounded by a forest. Bella hiked in the mountains of the ranch and knew there could be coyotes, mountain lions, bobcats, bears, and any number of predators. She had no idea where she was, but she couldn't just stand there either. She set off along the riverbank, glancing around as she walked. From the corner of her eye, she thought she saw something dark moving between the trees next to her. She stopped and peeked through branches, even moving to stand where she suspected she had seen something, but there was nothing. The feeling she was not alone remained, but she didn't sense danger—much.

The sound of the water rushing over rocks sent her back to the river. She knelt on the grass at the edge of a small, rounded curve where the clear, clean water pooled in a slow half-circle. The sight and the smell reminded her of the river back home. Maybe she was still at the ranch somewhere and had suffered a blackout of some sort. The last thing she remembered was gazing into the photo of where she was now. Her mind couldn't wrap its understanding around that at all. She definitely needed to find someone with answers.

She drank her fill of the cold water before she began walking along the river to her right.

Rounding a bend brought another surprise. A woman with long black hair and wearing a white dress soaked to the knees was walking in the center of the shallow water up to her calves. Her shoulders were slumped, and she was shaking her head slowly back and forth as though pondering something heavy on her heart. A small sob followed her forlorn sigh.

"Excuse me, dispénseme," Bella asked as she approached the lady. "Is there something I can do for you?"

The woman moved her head in a slow but deliberate turn toward Bella. Her hair hung in tangled waves down her back. The strands framing her face were white, however, and concealed part of her face. The part Bella could see showed a great sadness had befallen the poor woman which left one eye without hope and a mouth with the crease of a frown as though she had forgotten how to smile.

"I have lost my children." She spoke almost too softly to hear. "Mis niños se desapareceron en 'l agua. My babies disappeared into the water. I keep searching, and I walk in every stream I find. I long for the day I will find them again."

"Oh, I'm so sorry," Bella cried. She looked into the water, clear and flowing over and around rocks of varied sizes.

The woman waded forward through the stream again. Bella, trailing on the grassy bank, focused on the water and didn't notice the ease by which the woman walked without losing her balance on the moss-covered rocks. A normal person would be moving in a Frankenstein mimicry, flailing arms and all, over such slippery obstacles beneath the water. "I am doomed to look for them forever," the woman moaned.

"How long have you searched for them?"

"I do not know," the weeping woman replied. "Time is meaningless here."

"How do you know they are in this stream? Did you see them slip in?"

The woman stopped walking and turned her face toward Bella once more. "I know they are in the water," she said. "I do not know that they are in this particular stream, and so I search every body of water I find."

"But how d—"

"Because I drowned them!" the woman roared. She turned all the way then, her fists clenched at her sides. She tossed her long hair away from her face, and Bella saw the other eye, clouded with a white film as though blinded. The cheek over the mouth and to its side was open in a ragged-edged wound. It left her gums and teeth exposed in a caricature of a spectral smile.

"And if I cannot find my babies, I will be content to replace them with another," she growled and started toward Bella. No longer in the water, the Weeping Woman glided on top of it so fast that if Bella had hesitated, her adventure would have had a different end.

Bella's ear-piercing scream echoed through the valley long after she sprinted as far away from the river as she could. A small adobe house in the woods stopped her. She rushed inside and slammed the door behind her. A small table stood beside it. She yanked the *mesita* in front of the door and then turned around. Spotting a cot by the opposite wall, she slid beneath. She closed her eyes tight and heard someone say, "You are safe with me."

Bella's eyes flew open, and so did her mouth in a huge intake of breath, but she didn't move anything else. She mouthed an expletive her male cousins used. She peeked through the fringe of the bedspread and saw an old woman sitting in a rocker. The woman in whose home Bella had found refuge from the ghastly spirit threatening her was a curandera, Señora Matilde. She cured Bella from the susto she had sustained and warned, "Now that you have begun your little adventure, you know firsthand there is a bit of danger; you would do well to remain alert while you are here and figure out how to deal with each episode as it comes."

Bella reflected on what had sent her hiding here, to begin with. "How was I to know the lady in the river is a—a—what is she, anyway?"

"You do not know who she is?"

"Well, she didn't introduce herself, if that's what you mean."

"Do not be impertinent. No, that is not what I mean at all." The señora frowned. "Your parents, your grandparents—they never told you about the Weeping Woman?"

"No, no one."

"I see," the señora's eyes took on a faraway look for a moment. "She went by the name of María when she was alive. When she was a young woman, she made the mistake of falling in love with a man who was already betrothed to another. His intended bride and he were of the same kind— rich families, arranged marriage. No one knows whether the man seduced María or whether they gave in to a mutual attraction; in any case, she became pregnant. Again, no one knows whether she allowed it to happen to entrap him into marrying her. When he remained steadfast in keeping her in her place as his mistress even with the baby, she bore him another child, perhaps one more pitiful try to make him stay. The night of the man's marriage to the other woman, María lost her mind. She drowned her babies in the nearest river and then drowned herself. Now, she is known as la Llorona, the Weeping Woman. She is seen all over the southwest and Mexico haunting the rivers in her eternal search for her babies. Sometimes she, like a few others you will meet, returns to your world in the hopes she will be seen and her existence acknowledged once more. Rare are any sightings of them in your time though. Perhaps people do not look, or maybe they do not see because they are convinced the sight could never be real."

"How sad!"

"Yes, it is. But you would be wise to avoid running into her again. Some say she will replace her children with living ones if she gets her hands on any. That is the one person—er, spirit—you do not want to tempt. Solitary as she is, no one knows what she might do."

That was the first of many consejos Bella would get from those she met over the next few days. The advice, when she took it, kept her safe as she explored the woods on her own. She became familiar with some places, but she was escorted to others by some of the spirits she met. She learned to be watchful when she had to pass over the river or streams when she stopped for a drink and to fill the canteen Señora Matilde had given her.

The next occasion that brought la Llorona into her path happened after she had met the elder, Señor Montoya. They had finished their evening meal at his house and went for a walk to check on his small herd of cattle and to listen to the screaming of the frogs by the river. He assured Bella la Llorona wouldn't try anything with her with him around. The incident began with the action of another la—la Lechuza. A shapeshifting witch, she could turn into a giant owl and fly. Bella had met almost all who wanted to make themselves known to her except the giant pájaro and a few others.

Señor Montoya was standing a few feet from her with his back turned, his lantern raised high as he waited for his small herd of cows to join them. Bella's head was turned toward the opposite direction, her eyes in search of the owl whose hoots they had heard when they arrived at the river. The whoosh of large wings so close they blew cool air across Bella's back and head, as they passed, came so fast she had no time to duck. She felt smooth feathers brush up against her, but whatever it was disappeared into the dark, and she saw nothing. Señor Montoya was scratching the necks of the cows by that time, his attention on the ladies. It was obvious he had seen nothing. Apparently heard nothing either.

The second time Bella heard the hoots, she grew alert, her eyes above her, her body turning in all directions. The whooshing came close again, but she couldn't tell from which direction. She was in the act of turning in another spin when a wing caught her right in the middle of the back.

The thrust of the sudden push set Bella rushing straight ahead to keep her balance. Her forward motion, arms windmilling, took her over the riverbank. She fell on her knees, palms, and face-first into the water.

The "Aaaaah" coupled with the splash brought the old man to the water's edge. "¡Opale!" he uttered and held the lantern high. "¿Qué te pasó? What happened to you?"

Bella was spitting water and trying to stand but weighed down by her soaked clothing, she stumbled forward once more and fell on all fours again. The Weeping Woman rose to her waist from the water right in front of her. La Llorona smiled with the side of her mouth which could, and her hands reached out to Bella.

"Arghhh!" Bella screamed and backed up a few steps before turning to slip, stumble, and leap through the river. The water forced her to struggle ahead while the muddy river bottom sucked at her shoes. Bella felt as if the river had come to life and worked to keep her prisoner until la Llorona could touch her.

Señor Montoya's hand came from behind and yanked her by the shirt collar over the short bank. He let go quickly before he planted himself between her and the ghostly specter who now stood in the center of the flowing water. Bella was still tripping forward over fallen twigs and rocks and trying to stop without falling again. She caught her balance and then turned to look at the woman dressed in white. Though she was translucent, the features of her face were clear. Her mouth opened in an O, and the wailing emerged with such forlorn sadness had it been coming from any other woman, the sound would have torn any heart in two with pity. But it was la Llorona, the spirit of the woman who had performed the unthinkable—the murder of her children. She didn't generate much sympathy from people when their brains reminded their hearts of her plight. Her shoulders shook with her sobs as she turned with a defeated posture and glided through the water until her form was swallowed by the moonless night.

"¿Estas bien?" Señor Montoya had joined her and held the lantern up to see her better. "Vamos, pronto," he added when he saw water dripping from her hair into her face, her eyes wide in fright, and her teeth chattering with the shaking of her soaking wet body.

"Señor," Bella asked as they practically jogged to his house, "do you think la Lechuza is in cahoots with la Llorona. Do you think she pushed me into the river on purpose?"

The old man stopped short, holding the lantern high again to look into her eyes. Bella was the first living being to visit the land of the dead and the forgotten, el mundo de los olvidados. He wondered the same and opened his mouth to reply, but then he searched the moonless sky and said "apúrale" instead.

They hurried.

POETRY

Peacock-caffeine

by Zoltán Komor

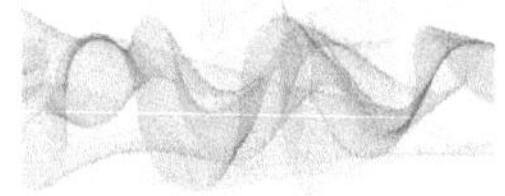

The girl with the carriage tongue wants to kiss
—I'll bet you've never seen anything like this
the chick's got an old-fashioned fiacre in her
mouth from the last century
—it's all silver, it's all gold— the kind of horse-
drawn four-wheeled carriage the leech-mustached
gentlemen in Vienna used to travel around
—she tells me this vehicle always runs toward her
front teeth carrying her unspoken words
—but never arrives—
maybe she wants to tell me love is a purposeless
journey
a kidnapped sunflower in a dark cellar, or a lonely
fat submarine hanging a hairy periscope in a men's
shower room
for a girl who doesn't have a real tongue, she does
talk a lot
— her words are mostly horse snorting's, the
chimes of Christmas bells and the crazy creaking
of wooden wheels— still, I understand that she's
chattering about the pits where the holes were

thrown, and these are the holes where the gaps
have fallen into,
and these are the gaps that make the abyss dizzy
—but all I care about is how to squeeze the caffeine
out of the peacocks—

the jellyfish of oblivion keep stinging my
forehead—
see, it's all covered with burning red rash now,
and every bump resembles a tired pearl diver
who has been suffering from a creative crisis for
years
and can only bring up bathtub plugs from the
bottom of the ocean instead of rare jewels
—sooner or later, they will drain all the water
—some say that urine is the best medicine for
jellyfish stings
because it's acidic and has ammonia in it
—but maybe the girl with the carriage tongue
would find it rather strange if I would piss myself
in the forehead right here and now
—although for a long time this was my favorite
hobby—
and before that, I also collected prison windows—
every morning, I wondered at the metal bars until
they started to disgust me
so, I have escaped from them and since then I
disguise myself as a free man

—my life was almost perfect until now,
but I need to find out how to squeeze the caffeine
out of peacocks

one of the wheels of the girl with the carriage
tongue falls off and rolls away,
Popping out of her mouth like a decaying tooth
—oh the mineral spark of suffering, the swollen
upper thigh of grief—mucous snails cling to each
other in the porcelain cupboard
—the wheel fracture of picturesque dreams—
maybe if I would have kissed this girl, her wheel
wouldn't have fallen out
—oh, dear girl with the carriage tongue, never
mind that damned fiacre
because your heart is all silver, it's all gold,
something that the leech-mustached gentlemen
would use to travel around in Vienna
—and I promise I'll hop into it and then we can
slide away, drawing a long blood stain in the snow
—and we'll take those cursed peacocks too —and
figure out how to squeeze all the caffeine out of
them on the way

Communion

by Vonnie Winslow Crist

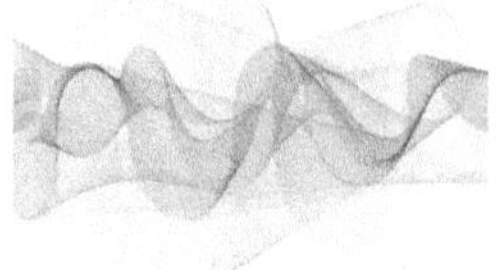

Right here, right now,
is that moment
when time pauses and friends gather,
when the grass beside the meeting house
bends in unison,
when oaks exhale,
and our lungs swell with sacred oxygen.

Right here, right now,
is that moment
when dust motes spin in holy light—
each speck a universe unto itself,
when air quickens with the hush
of willow roots parting earth
and worms burrowing underfoot,
when our furrowed palms
rub smooth walnut pews—
forgetting the sacrifice.

Right here, right now,
is that moment
when the dead press close,

separated from us by the sheerest gauze,
when we recognize the angelic
in the housefly tapping the windowpane,
when the wind slips through the doorway,
and the improbable seems possible.

Right here, right now,
is that moment
of peace, of miracle, of discovery.

How Can Time Travel Without Me in Tow

by Mark Heathcote

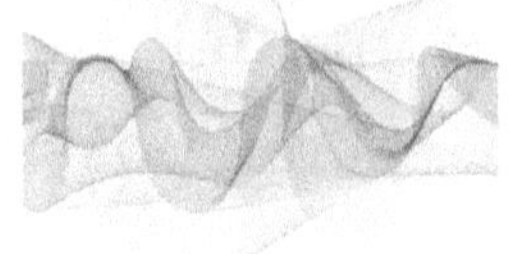

How can the night befall into starless
shadows?
If I-hold just-one in my heart as a guiding torch.
How can darkness descend and stop like a
tornado?
Or fall through a trapdoor - if I'm on your porch.

How can time travel without me in tow?
Am I not a part of its feathered falling arrow?
How can the wind leave my wings, my bow?
Leave without the one who caused my sorrow.

How can my heart just blatantly be stopped?
Did-I-not love you enough? Did-I-not armed
With my pen not write to you many a love song.
Wronged, am I now to fall stone-like aplomb?

Lord, when will I see fresh spring flowers again?
Catch those blossoms lost in their ragged fall.
Lord, when will I see that morning star attend?
Bestowing-light-on-me it's eternal-friend.

Corn Circles

by Mark Heathcote

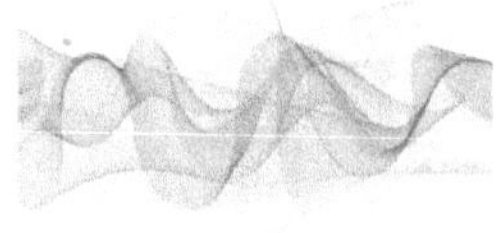

I'm not interested in corn circles
not even how you came to be.
All I've seen is flattened dejected people
Who'd once bathe your grazed soiled knee?

You may dance to your own celebrations
but please don't include me.
I've seen how your size 10 hobnail boots
have danced on their hearts and said amen.

I'm not interested in your accolades.
Only how you flattened all that golden wheat,
so proud you separated the wheat from the chaff
and left those dried-out familiar husks.

You may sing in the ranks of your own success
but please don't expect me to.
When you've forgotten all the lullabies sang
that once calmed a ferocious dark sea.

"The view from the sky sure is pretty" no doubt
and appealing to like-minded circling vultures.
But the bones-of-the-discarded can never be
forgotten.
Ultimately, they're how this feat came about.

Entomologist

by Mark Heathcote

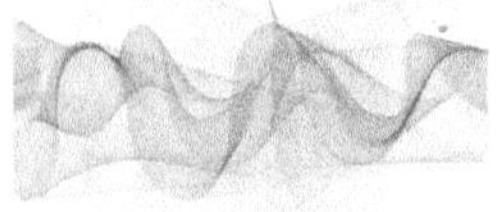

The way you are neglectful and uncaring
the way you dangle love as a lure to deceive
portraying an image of what is to procure
then snatch it away, is unforgiving.
Like a child who pulls off butterfly wings
hoping to stitch each membrane wound
to see it fly again.
An outward kiss blew inbound.
Like the Anglerfish,
it's the entomologist's way
to sheath what was beautiful.
Make it stay encased, grotesque.

On the Horizon

by John Drudge

Lost
In abstract
Imaginings of time
The strange peace
That comes
When there's nothing left
To be taken
In this restricted space
Of repetitive movement
Everything altered
Forever
Circumscribed and shackled
By seclusion
And the long seasonality
Of our waning
Lost on shores
Of relentless grieving
With only the faintest
Of lights
Left on the horizon
As we strive to rise
With ebbing tides
Of change
Together

Amongst the Stars

by Mike Turner

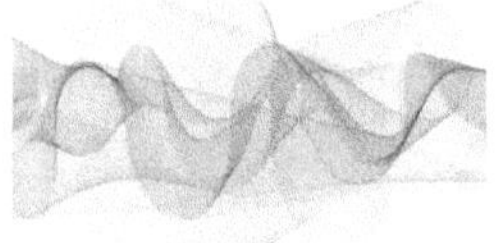

We are all but stardust
Individual protons, neutrons, electrons
Bound into atoms, nuclei, cells, muscle, bone,
organs
A living, breathing, walking shell we call "Human"

Surrounded by other stardust
The planet we live on comprised of
All the flora and fauna which sustain us
In this journey we call "Life"

When that journey concludes
We decompose back to essential elements
Returning at last again to stardust
In that process we call "Death"

Yet through this cycle
We are imbued with an additional force
One that animates us, gives us intellect, emotion
That ethereal thing we call "Soul"

And while stardust may be seen

In all its permutations: atoms, compounds
Planet, flora, fauna, human being
The Soul has no physical presence, but simply
"Is"

And just as our mortal bodies return
To the great teeming mass of the cosmos
So too do our Souls return
To merge in that spiritual Oneness to which we
ever belong

Amongst the stars

Unity: the Key to End Game

by Muskan Singh

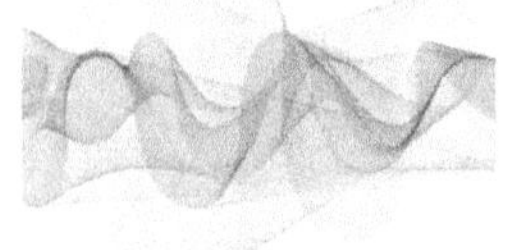

A simple five letter word,
Yet hidden with a deep meaning
Seen everywhere
Yet not fully understood

Whether it be an ant army of Ant-Man,
Or a colony of Wasp
Whether it be in bricks of Stark Tower,
Or in the Avengers themselves.

Unity can change the world,
It can save us from monsters like Thanos
Aake them vanish or hurled,
When it was all said and done.

When Divided they lost everything,
Lost stones, lost people, lost courage
When All united they won it back,
The people, the stones, and the War itself.

So, to stand strong and tall,
Alone you may be weak
But Unity is all,
Working like the roots of trees.

Mosquito

by Ross Jeffery

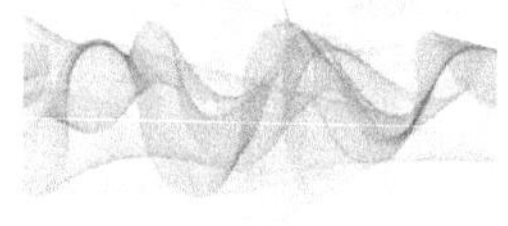

Her flesh is sapling fresh. Bruises at will.
I shouldn't but I couldn't . . . .
Hands grope, devour her throat, corrupt her flesh
for the last time. Bedaub her once radiant skin
with my unrelenting love of her.
I shouldn't but I couldn't . . . .
Gnarled tree root fingers find purchase, her
windpipe. She grows cold, my hands hot. They
sear her flesh. Brand her with my touch. Mark
her one last time in the most beautifully tragic of
ways.
I shouldn't but I couldn't . . . .
I hold her down within the crashing waves,
secluded amongst the rocks, hidden from the
revelers on the beach. Foaming waters muffle her
half-hearted whimpers of submission, eyes
fearful. Knowing. I hold her there, screams buried
deep within the slag heap of noise – hiding our
secret, our pact.
I shouldn't but I couldn't . . . .
A crack sounds within her fleshy prison of a neck.
Head lolls to the side. Struggles end. I let go.
She's at peace. Suspended in the ebbing tide,
back and forth, glassy eyed and pale skinned – if
the sea were amber she'd be my mosquito forever.
I shouldn't but I couldn't . . . .

'If I get cancer she said, the terminal kind, I want you to end it for me – cancer will not have this victory.'
I shouldn't but I did . . . .

Unchanged

by Vanessa Caraveo

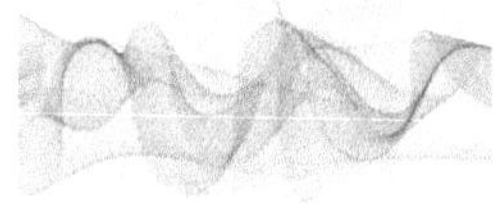

The bends of life come with challenges,
some may shake humans to their core,
Leaving them sad and broken.
Some may even be twisted and malformed,
leaving them untouched,
the way they always were.

Some seek a new horizon
to water the seeds of their dreams,
voices in some places scream at aliens,
while others welcome them with open arms,
confirming the irony of life and its people.
The newbies are called outcasts by some;
they tell them their ways are parallel.

The same land where some are seen as different
is the same that comforts land aliens.

They look strange to me,
dressed in those costumes.
Those were the thoughts of some,
forgetting we all come from differences
even though we share the same flesh and bones.

My way is a symbol of my beginning,
one that has always been a part of me since eons
ago.

No human transition can alter that,
the same way I won't alter yours.
And we all thrive when we mix and blend,
and strive to let all forms of enmity end.

The End of the World

by Michelle Chermaine Ramos

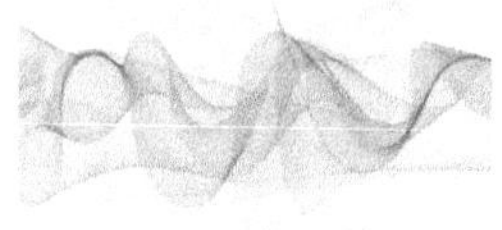

The stars began to die.
The sun came out from the west.
The cat played the fiddle.
Tadpoles sprang from a cuckoo's nest.
Hot dogs started barking.
The sea washed itself away.
Dandelions started roaring.
Spring sprang away.
My horse recited Shakespeare.
A frog now wears the crown.
Weeping willows wept an ocean.
Pigs flew high above the ground.
The rooster laid an egg.
The cow jumped over the moon.
Judging from these peculiar events,
The world will be ending soon.
The mouse chased the cat.
The waterfall ran uphill.

Now I've come to ask you…
Do you love me still?

Coat of Scars

by Tina Martinez

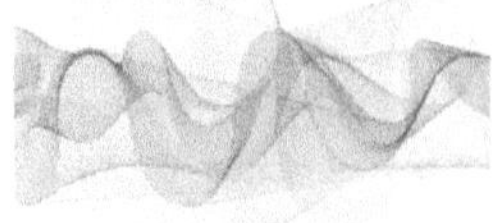

"How could I have known that my words cut deep?" he cried.
"I never meant you harm, you concealed your pain," she whimpered.
The Watchers took pity on us.
Pleading our case, petitioning for a naked truth
"Let them see the damage they inflict," The Watchers argued
"Their hearts will soften at the sight of manifested pain," They reasoned

As we slept, our shields were taken
Camouflaged veils dissipated like the morning fog

Those first hard remarks carelessly tossed at each other
Met with gasps of surprised pain
The sharp, red welts instantly rose up
Marred tender flesh left raw with transparent harm

Anger and cruelty

Gave rise to gashes that wept with exposed dolor
Truth, candor and honesty, while jarring to one's
ego
Induced stings and shocks, yet unbroken they
remained

Two factions were born that day
One thoughtful, yet honest
Solicitous and kind
Admired and sought after
Beautiful and incandescent to the naked eye

The others bore the trauma
Dealing blows in return
Circumvented and inflexible
Unable and unwilling to soften
Inevitably donning their coat of scars

Girl

by Michelle Brule

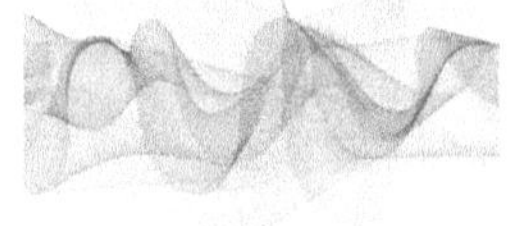

Needle pulling thread
fashioning seams
where your words
split me from myself.
The rawness
a compliment to your skill
your ability
to weaponize love.
Now my seamstress hands
undo the sutures
you stitched across my lips.
I must be quick
before I can
no longer
nourish myself.
As I break each one
undone
the scream inside me grows
and cannot be contained
in this millennium.
For those silenced in the past
for my sisters of the future
I scream
so, Justice will know
where to find us.

We All Went to the River

by Kurt Newton

We all went to the river
to drown ourselves in its mighty depths.
We stood on the banks
one by one ambling in.
The river took us by the ankles,
then by the legs,
until we were waist-deep,
our gowns billowing beside us
like blanched lily pads.
At last, the water grabbed us by the neck
and pushed us under,
once, twice, three times
into its bosom, making sure we tasted
its cool devouring nature.
And then it released us
to float downstream,
like pale boats seeking that speck of land
that called to us the loudest.
We washed ashore,
our bodies rich with purpose,
fingers grasping, gripping the land,
our feet once again

sinking into the soil.

The Summer We Died

by Kurt Newton

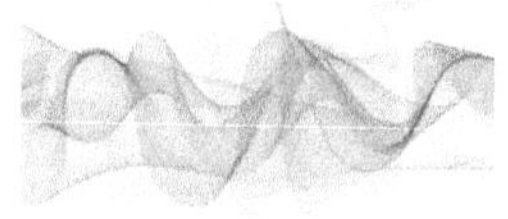

The summer we died,
we ignored the warnings,
we didn't go to work,
we spent all our money on drugs and alcohol.

The summer we died,
we threw great parties,
we drank till the sun came up,
we passed out and woke up with strangers.

The summer we died,
we let our children run free,
we let loose our animals,
we lost our phones and unplugged our television
sets.

The summer we died,
we didn't have time
to do all the things we wanted,
we did what we could, we made peace, we moved
on.

Coalition

by Maggie D Brace

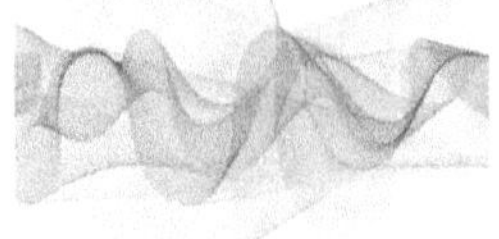

Cheek to cheek we join ourselves
as one unto the other.
The gills of me will sprinkle
the future spore of another.

With mycelium feet
we creep onward and onward.
A host of us joined up now
never letting our guard down.

The stem of you joins my gill cap,
luxuriating in our moist loam.
Our colony of one becomes
a mushroom universe home.

I Miss Community

by Sam M. Phillips

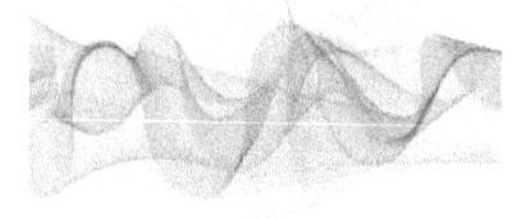

My computer is broken.
I can only make a token
Effort to fix it,
Might as well mix it
Amongst my other worries,
No one hurries
To solve them either.
Am I the driver
Of my own fate?

I hate
To take responsibility
For every calamity
That befalls me,
Stalls me
In my goals for life
But I guess strife
Brings challenge,
Forces us to change.
I just think it's strange
I'm meant to do it for self
Or it doesn't get done.

It's not any fun
Trying to be on top of things,
It brings no joy
To deploy myself to task,
It's too much to ask
Of just one person,
I'm certain
There's a better way.

I miss community,
That unity of effort
That helps us confront
A problem.
The conundrum
That we drum
Competition into everyone.
We've done
Ourselves a disservice,
It is not a vice
To do something nice
For someone at no gain to yourself.

Female of the Undergrowth

by Colin James

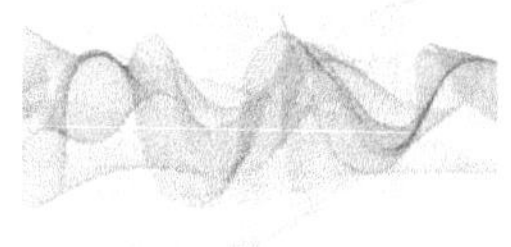

It's odd how my arms
involuntarily spread
when about to fall.
I never gave permission
to accept this risk,
would rather my Protestant arse
cushion my tactile parts
as told to a partial witness,
a fellow traveler in this quagmire
also suitably clad in camouflage
currently chasing me in the low brush.
I'm having difficulty keeping up
he seems to be outdistancing me.
For a second I thought I saw him
standing on the next small rise,
but that can't be possible since
I can hear his size fourteens
crushing the smaller plants
feel his breath on my ear. Then
who is that standing up there
hair groomed like an apocalypse?
It's the overdressed crucifixion, heroin.

A Moment in Time

by Darren B. Rankins

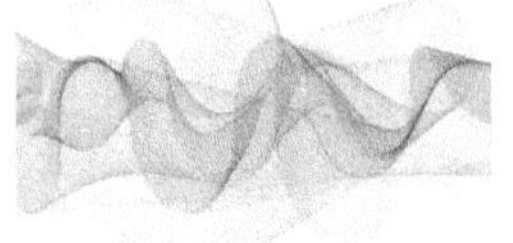

If you could see
your reflection
within the center
of my teardrops,

Or smell the scent of roses
within a summer breeze,

Then for one
moment in time,
you should realize
how much I love you.

Homeless

by Darren B. Rankins

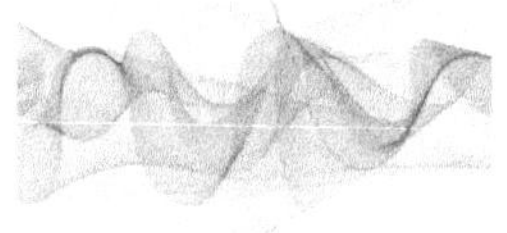

Just drifting
Without money, food,
And a place to sleep.
Homeless is
The only name I have.

Bubbles

by Darren B. Rankins

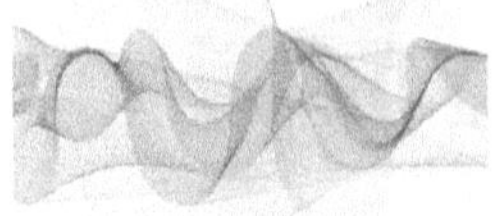

So perfect in shape
Decorated in rainbows
Soar toward heaven.

Missing Piece

by Mahanz Badihian

For all hard-working people around the World

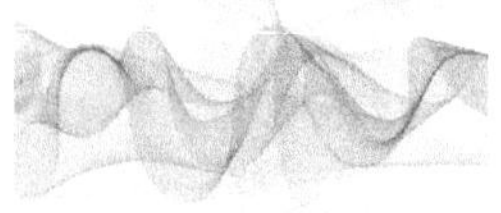

I wake up anxiously every day
not knowing what is rushing at
me through repeated moments.

Human love in the form that exists,
never been satisfying.
A love so limited, so incomplete,
that we easily lie, quickly kill, while
witnessing half of the World Suffer

We keep searching for
the missing piece in our life, but
in the end, we will give up and
settle with the absence of many
more pieces,

This is life, a precious whole
With lots of missing parts!

Eulogy for a Sandbox Universe

by Pedro Iñiguez

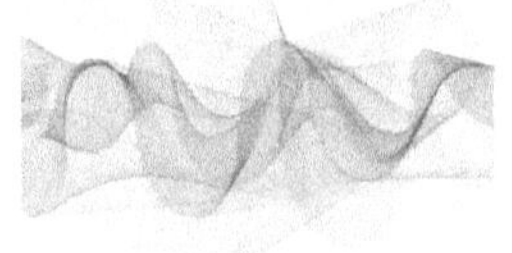

Creator:
Look again upon your box.
At that sea of dirt and gas and rocks.
Every twinkling grain,
a possibility: to expunge death and pain,
to walk back those blunders
and craft new wonders,
new people, new things,
worlds without fallen angels stripped of wings.
A chance to gather stardust and sculpt for us
your art,
that across these endless gulfs, there may be
luminous new starts.
Instead, you will your creations to love you and
loathe each other,
to wage war and pit brother against brother.
Most will shrivel and sink in the grit,
but those few left will climb from the pit,
and as the end of time unfurls,
they'll fly to the reaches of your world.
And just before they die,
they will find you, smile, and spit in your eye.

ART

Year Wheel

by Vonnie Winslow Christ

Winged Dragon

by Vonnie Winslow Christ

Man and Machine

by Vonnie Winslow Crist

Riding Triceratops

by Vonnie Winslow Crist

Alien Forest

by Vonnie Winslow Crist

Root 66

by Belinda Subraman

Nebula & Forest Floor

by Belinda Subraman

We Are the Landfill

by Jai Caldwell

Darkness Blind Us

by Michelle Chermaine Ramos

Darkness Bind Us by Michelle Chermaine Ramos

The Merry Cluster

by maggie de braces

Madame George

by Carlos Concha

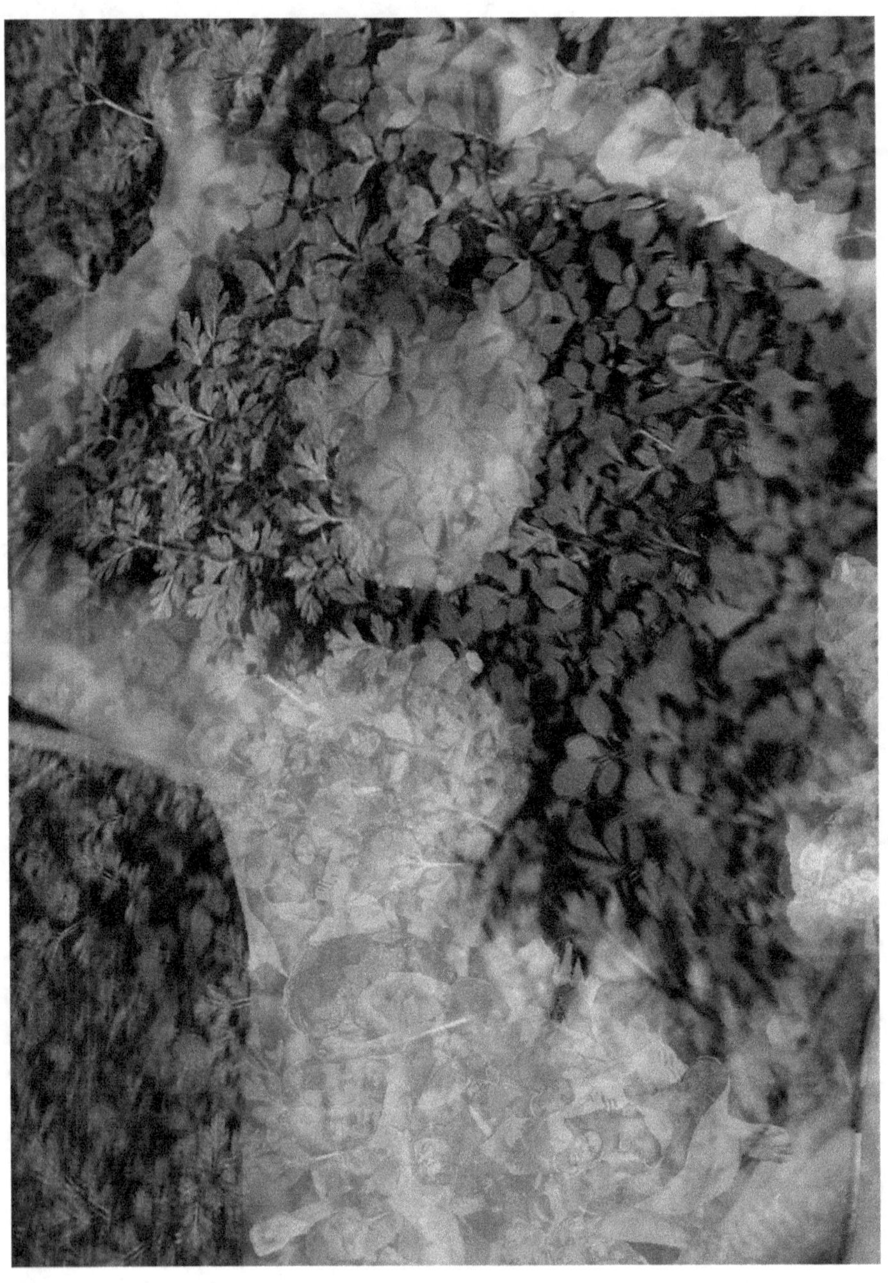

Cliff Brain

by Carlos Concha

Decay Den

by Mark Blickley

Acknowledgments

A special thanks to all the contributors from Penned in the City for supporting Doctors Without Borders with your contributions. Your generosity is boundless.

Also, thank you Daniel and Elaine for your editing expertise!

About the Artists and Authors

Fiction Authors

James Agombar J. Agombar resides near the treacherous waters of Southend-On-Sea, Essex, UK where visions of the speculative, criminal, and supernatural have taken over his mind (usually alongside a bottle of whisky). He holds a BA Hons in Humanities where the creative writing module inspired his first published work with Luna Press. He is a fan of the short story and is inspired by classic authors such as Richard Matheson, Ray Bradbury, and H.P Lovecraft. His work has been printed with over twenty publishers to date including two short story collections of his own. His third collection is in progress.

Carmen Baca taught high school and college English for thirty-six years before retiring in 2014. Her command of English and her regional Spanish dialect contribute to her story-telling style. Her debut novel *El Hermano* published in April 2017 and became a finalist in the NM-AZ book awards program in 2018. She has published four more books and 38 short works thus far in online literary magazines and anthologies. She and her husband live a quiet life in the country caring for their animals and any stray that happens to come by. You can learn more about her work at: http://plu.us/cbacacreations

Gabriella Balcom writes fantasy, horror, romance, sci-fi, and more, and has had 570 works accepted for publication. She was nominated for the Washington Science Fiction Association's Small Press Award, and Clarendon House Publications awarded her a publishing contract after one of her stories was voted best in a novel; her multi-genre anthology, *On the Wings of Ideas*, was then released. Gabriella won second place in JayZoMon/Dark Myth Company's 2020 Open Contract Challenge, and they published her romance, *Worth Waiting For*. Black Hare Press put out her sci-fi novella, *The Return*, and Dark Myth Publication released her horror anthology, *Down with the Sickness and Other Chilling Tales*. She also self-published a novelette. Her author page:

https://m.facebook.com/GabriellaBalcom.lonestarauthor

Elaine Marie Carnegie-Padgett, a paralegal, and private investigator also worked on the side as a newspaper journalist, history, and foodie columnist for a decade before accepting a publishing partnership; and then opening her own SPPublishing and Author Services. Publisher and Editor of the "Journeys" Anthology Series. She has worked with both the F.B.I. and Texas Rangers, and written for *Discovery ID on Human Trafficking*. Her articles have been published in both print and online venues, as well as in anthologies, charity, and collaborative projects. She makes her home in the idyllic East Texas Piney Woods doing what she loves and living her best life! You can find her online at https://www.authorelainemarie.com/

Vonnie Winslow Crist, SFWA, HWA, is the author of *The Enchanted Dagger, Owl Light, The Greener Forest,* and other award-winning books. Her stories appear in *Cast of Wonders, Amazing Stories, Lost Signals of the Terran Republic, Chilling Ghost Short Stories, Faerie Magazine, Cirsova Magazine,* and elsewhere. Her poems appear in *Sea Glass Hearts, Illumen, Weirdbook, Starward Tales II,* and elsewhere. For more information visit: www.vonniewinslowcrist.com

D.A. D'Amico

Dawn DeBraal lives in rural Wisconsin. She has published over 700 short stories, drabbles, and poems in online ezines and anthologies. She was a 2019 Pushcart nominee, awarded the international Literary Global Book Award for her first solo novel 2024, *The Lord's Prayer*, A Series of Horror, 2024 Weird Wide Web short story contest winner. She tends to lean toward the horror genre because it makes her life seem so much better. Dawn also writes under the pen name of Garrison McKnight.

https://www.facebook.com/All-The-Clever-Names-Were-Taken-114783950248991

https://linktr.ee/dawndebraal

https://www.amazon.com/stores/author/B07STL8DLX/allbooks

Christopher T. Dabrowski Christopher T. Dabrowski is a Polish writer and screenwriter. His books have been published in Poland, the USA, Canada, Spain, Germany and India. His stories were published in many countries: USA, England, Australia, Canada, Poland, Russia, Germany, India, Slovakia, Czech Republic, Brazil, Spain, Argentina, Italy, Hungary, Sweden, Mexico, Albania, Nigeria, Botswana, Zimbabwe, Tanzania, Uganda, Kenya, Costa Rica, Peru, Vietnam, Turkey, Ukraine, Romania, Portugal, Tunisia, Bosnia and Herzegovina, Bangladesh, Slovenia, South Korea, Austria, Central African Republic, Egypt, Columbia, Philippines, Nicaragua, Lithuania, Ireland, Indonesia, Denmark, Chile, Serbia, Democratic Republic of the Congo, Pakistan & amp; Kosovo.

Scott Russell Duncan (aka Scott Duncan-Fernandez) fiction involves the mythic, the surreal, the abstract, in other words, the weird. He is Indigenous-/Xicano/Anglo from California, Texas, and New Mexico and is a senior editor at *Somos en Escrito Literary Magazine*. In 2016 he won San Francisco Lit-quake's Short Story Contest. His piece "Mexican American Psycho is in Your Dreams" won first place in the 2019 Solstice Literary Magazine Annual Literary Contest. See more about his work, publications, and "Quasi-Vato" blog on Scott's website scottrussellduncan.com.

Frangipanni graduated with an M.A. in Creative Writing from Sheffield Hallam University in 2015. Her short stories have been informed by her world travels exhibiting as an artist and presenting published papers at various international conferences. Many of her magic realism short stories, infused with cultural folklore, center around greater care of the natural and urban environment. Her creative memoir focuses on her female dual heritage, Chinese and English, in Britain. She has won various writing awards such as a *Resurgence* magazine competition and Bi'An runner-up award for Chinese writers in Britain. In 2010, she was awarded an art-practiced-based Ph.D. from Manchester Metropolitan University. You can learn more about her writing happenings at http://frangipanniwrites.com/index.html

Miriam H. Harrison Writing from the boreal forests and abandoned mines of Northern Ontario, Miriam H. Harrison writes poetry and fiction varying between the eerie, the dreary, and the cheery. Updates about her published works can be found on Facebook (https://www.facebook.com/miriam.h.harrison) or her website (https://miriamhharrison.wordpress.com/).

Pedro Iñiguez, originally from Los Angeles, now lives in Sioux Falls, South Dakota. He spends most of his time reading, writing, and painting, which stems from his childhood love of Science-Fiction, Horror, and comic books. His work can be found in various magazines and anthologies such as *Space and Time Magazine, Crossed Genres, Dig Two Graves, Writers of Mystery and Imagination, Deserts of Fire,* and *Altered States II.* His cyberpunk novel *Control Theory* and his 10-year collection *Synthetic Dawns & Crimson Dusks* can be found online. Currently, he is working on his second novel. He can be found online at pedroiniguezauthor.com.

Ross Jeffrey's fiction has appeared in various print anthologies and his short stories and flash fiction have been published in many online magazines. He lives in Bristol with his wife (Anna) and two children (Eva and Sophie). You can follow him on Twitter here @Ross1982.

Raync King

Zoltán Komor was born on June 14, 1986. He lives in Nyiregyhaza, Hungary. He writes surreal short stories and is published in several literary magazines (*Horror, Sleaze and Trash; Drabblecast; The Phantom Drift; Gone Lawn; Bizarro Central; Bizarrocast; Thrice Fiction Magazine; The Missing Slate; The Gap-Toothed Madness; Wilderness House Literary Re-view; Kafka Review*, etc.) His first English book, titled *Flamingos in the Ashtray: 25 Bizarro Short Stories*, was released by Burning Bulb Publishing in 2014, his second, titled *Tumour djinn* was released by Morbidbooks in the same year, and his third collection, *Turd Mummy* was released by Strange House Books in 2016.

Kevin Lauderdale's work has appeared in several of Pocket Books' *Star Trek* anthologies, the journal *Nature*, and a handful of genre / "new weird" anthologies.

Madeleine McDonald lives in Yorkshire, England, and finds inspiration walking on the beach. Her work has been broadcast on BBC radio and published in anthologies or journals. Her historical novel, *A Shackled Inheritance*, is available on Amazon Kindle.

Kurt Newton's Kurt Newton's writings have appeared in *Unity, Vol. I, The Fabulist, Cafe Irreal, Extra Sensory Overload, and Katabatic Circus. His poetry collection, THE BODY SNATCHERS & Other Death Rituals*, was recently published by Island of Wak-Wak. Another collection, *MOONLIGHT APOCRYPHA*, will appear later this year, also from Island of Wak-Wak.

Isabelle Palerma lives in the Midwest but fantasizes about running away to Florence, Italy someday. She writes poetry as well as fiction. Isabelle loves going on hikes, singing along, and dancing at concerts, traveling, and is a secret adrenaline junkie. She's been writing since she was seven, but fortunately, most of her early writing about talking dogs and dancing gumdrops have faded into obscurity.

Beth W. Patterson was a full-time musician for over two decades before diving into the world of writing, a process she describes as "fleeing the circus to join the zoo". She is the author of the books *Mongrels and Misfits* and *The Wild Harmonic*, and a contributing writer to over ninety anthologies. Patterson has performed in over twenty countries, collecting lore. Her playing appears on over two hundred albums, singles, soundtracks, commercials, and voice-overs (including nine solo albums of her own).

Select works of her fiction is archived in the Lunar Codex, an international lunar time capsule.

www.bethpattersonmusic.com

www.facebook.com/bethodist

www.instagram.com/bethodist_manifesto/

Sam Phillips is the co-founder of Zombie Pirate Publishing. He has had over 150 of his own short stories, articles, and poems published in anthologies and magazines around the world. His debut short novel appears in *Science Fiction Double Feature: Phosphorus & Into the Eye*. He has recently published his debut collection of stories, *Infinity and I: Seventy Science Fiction Stories*. Find out more about his publishing and books at Zombie Pirate Publishing's website:

www.zombiepiratepublishing.com You can also read his poetry and fiction on his blog:

www.bigconfusingwords.wordpress.com

Anthony Self

Paula Shablo is an American writer. Born in Idaho, her family moved to Wyoming when she was six, and she lived there many years before making Colorado her home.

Paula has loved writing stories since childhood, but it took a pushy son to persuade her to give publishing a shot.

Mother of four, grandmother of ten, and great grandmother of two, she's happiest when surrounded by family and friends.

Paula is an avid reader and a staunch supporter of public libraries.

US Amazon Author Page:
https://www.amazon.com/Paula-Shablo/e/B01H2HJBHQ
UK Amazon Author Page:
https://www.amazon.co.uk/Paula-Shablo/e/B01H2HJBHQ
Blog: http://paulashablo.com
Vocal Media: Paula Shablo | Vocal
Medium: Paula Shablo – Medium

Poetry Authors

Michelle Chermaine Ramos is a versatile Canadian artist, author, and journalist of Filipino-Spanish-Japanese descent. Her creative journey spans a wide spectrum, encompassing fine arts, acting, jewelry design, and literary pursuits.

Drawing inspiration from her multicultural roots, her work is a tapestry of influences that reflect her vibrant personal narrative. Her formative years spent in the Middle East, along with her deep fascination for various cultures and faiths, have shaped her artistic vision. Through her art, she aims to bridge cultural divides and encourage a deeper appreciation of our shared human experience.

Her dedication to promoting understanding doesn't stop with her art. Her career has encompassed roles as a TV/radio host and print reporter with a special focus on covering news in the areas of art, culture, entertainment, martial arts, social justice, business, and other matters of interest to immigrant communities in Canada. An inspirational storyteller, she has interviewed and spotlighted the success stories of local and global trailblazers, creatives, and entrepreneurs.

Connect with her online:
- Instagram: @michellechermaine
- Facebook: http://www.facebook.com/MichelleChermaineArt/
- Website: http://www.michellechermaine.com
- E-mail: info@michellechermaine.com

Vanessa Caraveo is an award-winning bilingual author, published poet, and artist who has a passion for promoting inclusion, empowerment and equality for all, helping others discover the power they possess within themselves to overcome adversity and persevere in life. She is involved with various organizations that assist children and adults with disabilities and enjoys working with nonprofit groups and volunteering in the promotion of literacy. Her work has been published in *Literature Today Journal, Poetrybay, The Raven Review, Anacua Literary Arts Journal,* and in various anthologies throughout the years.

Vonnie Winslow Crist, SFWA, HWA, is author of *The Enchanted Dagger, Owl Light, The Greener Forest,* and other award-winning books. Her stories appear in *Cast of Wonders, Amazing Stories, Lost Signals of the Terran Republic, Chilling Ghost Short Stories, Faerie Magazine, Cirsova Magazine,* and elsewhere. Her poems appear in *Sea Glass Hearts, Illumen, Weirdbook, Starward Tales II,* and elsewhere.
For more information: www.vonniewinslowcrist.com

John Drudge Growing up in both Canada and the Bahamas, John's upbringing has bestowed upon him a deep appreciation for the beauty of nature and the diversity of cultures. A dedicated M.S.W. social worker, successful entrepreneur, and Disability Management Specialist, John's educational journey has been one of unwavering commitment to others, having earned undergraduate and graduate degrees in social work, rehabilitation services, and psychology.

Beyond his academic pursuits, John's passions also extend to the martial arts. With a third-degree black belt in Kenpo Karate, he embodies discipline, perseverance, and a thirst for self-improvement. The martial arts have not only shaped his mind and body but also mirror his approach to life – a holistic journey towards balance and mastery.

He is the author of four books of poetry: *March* (2019), *The Seasons of Us* (2019), *New Days* (2020), and *Fragments* (2021), and his work has appeared widely in numerous literary journals, magazines, and anthologies internationally. John is also a Pushcart Prize and Best of the Net nominee and lives in Caledon Ontario, Canada with his wife and two children.

Mark Andrew Heathcote is an adult learning difficulties support worker. His poems have been published in journals, magazines, and anthologies online and in print. He is from Manchester and resides in the UK. Mark is the author of *In Perpetuity* and *Back on Earth*, two books of poems published by Creative Talents Unleashed.

Pedro Iñiguez, originally from Los Angeles, now lives in Sioux Falls, South Dakota. He spends most of his time reading, writing, and painting, which stems from his childhood love of Science-Fiction, Horror, and comic books. His work can be found in various magazines and anthologies such as *Space and Time Magazine, Crossed Genres, Dig Two Graves, Writers of Mystery and*

Imagination, Deserts of Fire, and *Altered States II*. His cyberpunk novel *Control Theory*, and his 10-year collection *Synthetic Dawns & Crimson Dusks* can be found online. Currently, he is working on his second novel. He can be found online at https://pedroiniguezauthor.com/

Colin James has a couple of chapbooks of poetry published. *Dreams Of the Really Annoying* from Writing Knights Press and *A Thoroughness Not Deprived of Absurdity* from Piski's Porch Press and a book of poems, *Resisting Probability*, from Sagging Meniscus Press.

Tina Martinez Tina Martinez is a native of Northern New Mexico, and a single mother to two amazing daughters. She holds a bachelor's degree in Creative Writing from the University of New Mexico, and a master's degree in Educational Leadership from New Mexico Highlands University. Tina retired from the public school system in 2024 after serving 25 years as a dual-language teacher, elementary school principal and district resource for Adult Education. In her retirement, she is enjoying spending time with her family, traveling, home remodeling projects, yoga, and is serving on a school board of a local charter school. Tina's written work includes a bilingual children's book, various short stories, and poetry.

Darren B. Rankins began his writing career in sixth grade and became excited about poetry when the MTSU

Honors Program Director suggested that Darren take part in the 1994 MTSU Poetry Slam. He has since had publications in several magazines and newspapers. E: Purethoughts24@yahoo.com W: www.purethoughts.info

Mike Turner is a poet/songwriter living on the US Gulf Coast. He has more than 400 poems published in over 100 literary journals/sites and anthologies; his book, *Visions and Memories*, was published in 2021 by Sweetycat Press and is available on Amazon. Mike was featured performing his original songs about the Gulf Coast at the 2021 Monroeville Literary Festival; his lyric, "Sense of Peace", was awarded the 2023 Roger Williams Peace Prize by the Alabama Writers' Cooperative.

Artists

Maggie D Brace, a life-long denizen of Maryland, teacher, gardener, basketball player and author attended St. Mary's College, where she met her soulmate, and Loyola University, Maryland. She has written '*Tis Himself: The Tale of Finn MacCool* and *Grammy's Glasses*, and has multiple short works and poems in various anthologies. She remains a humble scrivener and avid reader.

Jai Caldwell. I am Jai, but you can call me The Rooski. Young, Black, womxn dedicated to the craft that is causing confusion and admiration through creative endeavors like art or creative writing! Wish my audience love and light!

Mark Blickley grew up within walking distance of New York's Bronx Zoo. He is a proud member of the Dramatists Guild and PEN American Center. His latest book is the flash fiction collection *Hunger Pains* (Buttonhook Press).

Vonnie Winslow Crist, SFWA, HWA, is author of *The Enchanted Dagger, Owl Light, The Greener Forest,* and other award-winning books. Her stories appear in *Cast of Wonders, Amazing Stories, Lost Signals of the Terran Republic, Chilling Ghost Short Stories, Faerie Magazine, Cirsova Magazine,* and elsewhere. Her poems appear in *Sea Glass Hearts, Illumen, Weirdbook, Starward Tales II,* and elsewhere.
For more information visit: www.vonniewinslowcrist.com

Norbert Somosi (or shortly NoSo) is a Romanian artist, mostly creating surrealistic and imaginative works. His compositions are created tradition-ally by hand, in a unique style with pen and ink, and explore a variety of themes. His drawings try to conceptualize human experiences, experiences that are sometimes hard to put into words that are taboo or not very much discussed openly in our society. He seldomly does compositions in a traditional sense like portraits, landscapes, or still life. His focus and thinking are more like that of a writer. There is a story and interaction in most of his drawings.

He has illustrated books before (ex. *Hungry Thing* written by Shawn M. Klimek), but he doesn't consider himself as an illustrator. He is a storyteller with images, where the viewer is invited to create his or her per-sonal narrative.

Besides writing and publishing for decades **Belinda Subraman** was a Registered Nurse for 14 years, mostly in hospice. She's also an artist working in ink and acrylics. Belinda's art and poetry have appeared in many publications both online and in print. She is editor and publisher of *GAS: Poetry, Art and Music*, an online zine and video show as well as a group on Facebook. She also video interviews poets and artists for *GAS* and *Beatlife* ezines.

About the Editors

DANIEL BROOKS is from Indianapolis, Indiana. He is a special education teacher. His work has appeared or is forthcoming in the *Indianapolis Review*, *People's Tribune*, *Hawai'i Review*, and more.

ELAINE MARIE CARNEGIE-PADGETT, a paralegal, and private investigator also worked on the side as a newspaper journalist, history, and foodie columnist for a decade before accepting a publishing partnership; then opening her own SPPublishing and Author Services. She has worked with both the FBI and Texas Rangers, written for *Discovery ID on Human Trafficking.* Her articles have been published in both print and online venues, as well as in anthologies, charity, and collaborative projects. She makes her home in the idyllic East Texas Piney Woods doing what she loves and living her best life! You can find her online at https://www.authorelainemarie.com/.

MARIA J. ESTRADA is an English college professor at Harold Washington College. In the summer of 2020, she founded Barrio Blues Press. The mission of Barrio Blues Press is to elevate the voices of emerging writers and to help build a cooperative society through writing. She lives in Chicago's south side with her supportive husband, two remarkable children, and two mischievous cats. This work is the second charity book published by Barrio Blues Press. The proceeds are going to Doctors Without Borders. You can learn more about upcoming projects from Barrio Blues Press at barrioblues.com.

BOOKS BY BARRIO BLUES PRESS

Nation: A Poetry Book by Penned in the City

Available on Amazon for $5.99 in paperback & $1.99 Kindle/KU.

All proceeds go to the Chicago Freedom School.

Unity, Volume 1: A Magical Realism Anthology

Available on Amazon for $9.99 in paperback &
$5.99 Kindle/KU.

All proceeds go to Doctors Without Borders.

9 781954 444058